"I don't need you to save me."

"That's not what this is." But even as he said it, he wasn't entirely sure that was the truth. He didn't think about it in terms of saving her. He thought about it in terms of *helping*. Of course, why he felt this compulsion to help Kate was another question that he didn't want to investigate too deeply right now.

"Then tell me what this is about. The truth, Seth."

The truth? Hell. The truth was he was worried about her. He couldn't stop fantasizing about her. He was glad that she hadn't married Roger. He knew how hard single mothers had it and he didn't want it to be that hard for her. It shouldn't be that hard for anyone, but especially not for her.

He didn't say any of that. Instead, he closed the distance between them and cupped her face in his hands. "This," he said, lowering his lips to hers, "is the truth."

Little Secrets: Claiming His Pregnant Bride

SARAH M. ANDERSON

MAGNA 25/8/1 +

First published in Great Britain 2017
By Mills & Boon, an imprint of HarperCollins*Publishers*
1 London Bridge Street, London, SE1 9GF

Large Print edition 2017

© 2017 Sarah M. Anderson

ISBN: 978-0-263-07216-7

Printed and bound in Great Britain
by CPI Antony Rowe, Chippenham, Wiltshire

Sarah M. Anderson may live east of the Mississippi River, but her heart lies out west on the Great Plains. Sarah's book *A Man of Privilege* won an RT Reviewers' Choice Best Book Award in 2012. *The Nanny Plan* was a 2016 RITA® Award winner for Contemporary Romance: Short.

Sarah spends her days having conversations with imaginary cowboys and billionaires. Find out more about Sarah's heroes at sarahmanderson.com and sign up for the new-release newsletter at eepurl.com/nv39b.

To everyone who stood up for
what they believed.
You continue to inspire me!

One

Of all the things Seth Bolton wanted to be doing today, attending the wedding of a guy he went to college with was pretty low on the list.

Besides, he hadn't even liked Roger Caputo. Seth had been forced to live with Roger for three hellish months in college when Seth's roommate had backed out and Seth had been desperate to cover the rent without asking his family for help. That Roger had been a senior and unable to get any roommate but a freshman should have been the first clue to how Seth's three months were going to go.

It wasn't that Roger was a bad guy—he was just a jerk. Entitled, spoiled, inconsiderate—every privileged white-guy stereotype rolled into one. That was Roger.

Seth couldn't imagine who was foolish enough to marry Roger, but clearly someone was. Seth had no idea if he should pity this woman or not.

He gunned the engine up the incline, following the road as it snaked through the Black Hills. The wedding was supposed to start at five thirty—Seth was running late. It was already five forty and he had at least fifteen miles to go.

For some reason, the wedding was being held at a resort deep in the Black Hills, forty minutes away from Rapid City.

Why did people have destination weddings? Well, he knew why. The late-summer sun was already lower in the sky, casting a shimmering glow over the hills. They weren't black right now, not with the sun turning them golden shades of orange and red and pink at the edges.

It was *pretty*—not that he was looking as he took the next curve even faster. Roger must've found one hell of a woman if she wanted to tie herself to him with all this beauty around her.

Or maybe the jerk had changed. It was possible. After all, Seth himself had once been the kind of impulsive, restless kid who'd stolen a car and punched a grown man in the face because the man had dared to break Seth's mother's heart. Sure, that man—Billy Bolton—had married his mother and adopted Seth, despite the punch. But still, that was the sort of thing Seth used to be capable of.

Maybe he was still a little impulsive, he thought as he flew down the road well over the speed limit. And yeah, he was definitely still restless. The last year living in Los Angeles had proved that. But he'd gotten good at controlling his more destructive tendencies.

So people could change. Maybe Roger had become a fine, upstanding citizen.

The road bent around an outcropping, and Seth leaned into the curve, the Crazy Horse chopper rumbling between his legs. This was a brand-new model, in the final stages of testing, and he was putting it through its paces. The new engine had throwback styling combined with modern power and a wider wheelbase. The machine handled beautifully as he took another curve and leaned in hard. Seth felt a surge of pride—he'd helped design this one.

Damn, he'd missed these hills, the freedom to open up the throttle and ride it hard. LA traffic made actually riding a chopper a challenge. And palm trees had nothing on the Black Hills.

His father and his uncles, Ben and Bobby Bolton, owned and operated Crazy Horse Choppers, a custom chop shop in Rapid City, South Dakota. Crazy Horse had been founded by their father, Bruce Bolton, but the Bolton brothers had taken the company from a one-man shop in Bruce's garage in the early eighties to a company with sixty employees and a quarter of a billion in sales every year.

Seth had never had a father growing up, never expected that he would be a part of any family business. But when Billy adopted Seth ten years ago, the Bolton men had embraced him with open arms.

And now? Seth was a full partner in Crazy Horse Choppers.

He still couldn't get his head around the meeting yesterday. His dad and uncles had called him into the office and offered him an equal share in Crazy Horse. And Seth was no idiot. Of course he'd said yes.

At the age of twenty-five, he was suddenly a millionaire. A *multimillionaire*. Considering how he and his mom had sometimes been on welfare when he was a little kid, it was a hell of a shock.

But Seth knew it wasn't straight nepotism—he worked hard at making Crazy Horse Choppers a successful business. He'd just gotten back from living in Los Angeles for a year, managing the Crazy Horse showroom and convincing every A-to D-list celebrity that a Crazy Horse chopper was good for their image. And he'd excelled at the job, too. Getting Rich McClaren to ride up the red carpet at the Oscars on a Crazy Horse chopper—right before he won the award? Seth's idea. The free advertising from that had boosted sales by eight percent overnight.

The McClaren stunt was the kind of strategic thinking that Seth did now. He didn't just react—and react poorly. He planned. The best defense was a good offense.

Even now—he wasn't just going to a former friend's wedding. A quick internet search had revealed that Roger was a real estate agent now, part owner in his own agency. He was up-and-coming in the civic world of Rapid City. And after a year in LA, Seth was back in Rapid City. Maybe even permanently.

Seth was not going to this wedding to wish Roger and his new bride happiness, although he would. Seth was going to the wedding because he planned to be an up-and-comer himself. God knew that he had the money now.

The Bolton men might have given him a place at the table, but Seth was going to damn well keep it.

He screamed around a curve but saw something that made him ease off the throttle. There was a limo at a scenic overlook—but something wasn't right. Seth couldn't brake fast enough to stop without crashing, but he slowed enough to get a better look.

Something was definitely wrong. The limo was parked at a crazy angle, its bumper hanging in the roadway. Was there someone behind the wheel? He didn't see anyone enjoying the view.

He was late—but he couldn't in good conscience ride on. Seth pulled a U-turn on the road and headed back to the overlook. Did his phone even have service out here? Because if this wasn't some crazy wedding photographer stunt and the driver was having an emergency...

The limo was still running when Seth pulled up alongside it. His heart leaped in his throat when he realized that the front wheel on the passenger side wasn't exactly on solid ground. The driver had stopped just before the wheel went off the edge of the overlook completely. Hitting the gas would mean certain death.

He hopped off the bike and hurried to the driver's side. He hadn't been wrong—there *was* someone behind the wheel. A woman. Wearing a wedding dress and a…tiara?

Definitely not the limo driver.

She wasn't crying, but her eyes were wide as she stared at nothing in particular. Her color was terrible, a bluish shade of gray, and she had what appeared to be a death grip on the steering wheel. Basically, she looked like someone had shot her dog. Or ruined her wedding.

For all of that, she was quite possibly the most beautiful woman he'd ever seen.

How many brides were wandering around this part of South Dakota? Was this Roger's bride? If so, what was she doing *here*? Where was Roger?

He knocked on the glass of the driver's-side door. "Ma'am?" he said in what he hoped was a comforting voice. "Could you roll down the window?"

She didn't move.

"Excuse me? Ma'am?" This time, he tried the handle. Miracle of miracles, the door was not locked. When he opened it, she startled and swung her head around to look at him. As she did so, the limo shuddered. "Where did you come from?"

"Hi," Seth said in a soothing voice, hanging on to the door as if that could keep the car from plummeting off the side of the hill. "I'm going to turn this off, okay?"

Her eyes blinked at different speeds. "What?"

Seth leaned into the limo, keeping an eye on her in case she started to freak out. The limo was actually in Park, thank God. She must have taken her foot off the brake when he startled her. "I'm Seth," he told her, pulling the key from the ignition. "What's your name?"

Seth didn't expect her to burst out laughing as if he had told a joke. Clearly, this was a woman whose actions could not be predicted. Then, as quickly as she'd started laughing, the sound died in the back of her throat and she made a strangled-sounding sob. "I'm not sure."

Bad sign. He had to get her out of the limo. "Can you come talk to me? There's a bench over there with a great view of the sunset." He tried to make it sound like he was just here for the vista.

"You not going to tell me to get married, are you?"

Seth shook his head. "You're here for reasons. All of those reasons—I bet they're good ones."

She blinked at him again, her brow furrowed. He could see that she was coming back to herself now. "Are you here for a reason, too?"

He gave her a reassuring smile. "Everything happens for a reason."

This time, when she started laughing, he was ready for it. He chuckled along with her as if they were at a comedy club in downtown LA as opposed to on the edge of a scenic overlook in the Black Hills. He held out a hand to her and bowed at the waist. "Seth Bolton, at your disposal."

For the longest second, she just stared at him, as if he were a *Tyrannosaurus rex* that had emerged from the undergrowth and was roaring at her. "I'm not imagining you, right? Because you're kind of perfect and I made a mess of everything."

"I'm very real—the last time I checked, anyway," he joked, which got a small, quick smile out of her. He kept his hand out, the picture of a chivalrous gentleman. *Take it*, he thought. He would feel so much better if she were on solid ground next to him.

She placed her hand in his and it took everything he had not to close his fingers around hers and yank her out of the driver's seat—and into his arms. Instead, he tightened his grip on her ever so slightly and waited as she swung her feet out and stood. Her layers of dress settled around her—silk and satin and chiffon and all of those fabrics that his aunt Stella made dresses out of for her fashion line.

He didn't think this was one of Stella's dresses. Stella designed classic gowns that looked deceptively simple. This gown?

There wasn't anything simple about it. The bride looked a little bit like an overdone cupcake, with sparkles and sprinkles. The skirt was huge, with tiers and layers of ruffles and lace. How had she even fit behind the wheel in that monstrosity?

Her golden-brown hair was swept up into some elaborate confection that matched the dress, but at some point it had tilted off its bearings and now listed dangerously to the left. Pearls dripped off her ears and around her neck, but her ring finger was bare.

What did she look like when she wasn't dressed up like a bride? All he could see of her was her face and her bare shoulders. And her cleavage, which was kind of amazing—not that he was looking. His body tightened with awareness even as he tried to focus on her eyes. It didn't help, staring down into her face. Everything tugged him toward her with an instinctive pull that wasn't something he'd planned on, much less could control.

His first instinct had been right—she was gorgeous, he realized as she lifted her gaze to his. A sweetheart face, wide-set eyes that were the deepest shade of green he'd ever seen. The kind of eyes a man could get lost in, if he weren't careful.

Seth was careful. *Always.*

He knew exactly what happened when a man lost his head around a woman. So it was final—

no losing himself in her eyes. Or any other of her body parts. She might be a goddess, but she was obviously having a very bad day and he wasn't about to do a single damn thing that would make it worse.

So he locked down this intense awareness of her.

She wasn't for him. All he could—and should—do was offer her a helping hand.

"Hi." He launched another smile, one that had broken a few hearts, in her direction. "I'm Seth," he repeated because he honestly wasn't sure if she'd processed it the first time.

"Kate," she replied in a shaky voice. She hadn't pulled her hand away from his yet. Seth took an experimental step back—away from the limo—and was pleased when she followed. "I…I'm not sure what my last name is right now. I don't think I got married. I'm pretty sure I left before that part."

In his time, Seth had seen people involved in accidents still walking and talking and functioning almost normally because they were in a complete state of shock. Big dudes thrown from choppers and yet walking around and cracking jokes with one of their arms hanging out of the socket. Later, when the adrenaline had worn off, they'd felt the pain. But not at first.

Was this what this was? Had she been hurt? He looked her over as surreptitiously as he could, but he didn't see any injuries—so this was just a mental shock, then.

"Kate," he said, his voice warm and friendly. "That's a pretty name. What would you like your last name to be?

"Burroughs," she said firmly. "I don't want to be Kate Caputo. I can't be."

Seth let out a careful breath. That answered that question.

He had found Roger's runaway bride.

Two

Kate felt like she was moving in a dream. Everything was blurry at the edges—but getting sharper. How much time had she lost? A couple of hours? A couple of days? The last thing she remembered was...

She had been sitting in the little room set aside for the bride to get ready, staring at the mirror and fighting back the rising tide of nausea. Because she was pregnant and she was supposed to be marrying Roger and—and—

"Easy," a strong, confident male voice said.

She looked down to see that her hand was being

held by a man who was *not* Roger and they were *not* at the lodge she had especially selected for the beautiful sunset. She looked around, startling again. None of this looked familiar. Especially not him. She'd remember him. "I don't…"

The man's arm went around her waist and even though she didn't know who he was or what was going on, she leaned into his touch. It felt right—comforting. *Safe.* Whoever he was, he was safe. Maybe it was all going to be okay. She could have cried with relief.

"I've got you," he said, sounding so very calm when there was nothing to be calm about. "It's all right."

She laughed at that. "No, it's not."

"It's not as bad as you think, I promise. Roger will get over this, and so will you."

She wasn't sure she believed that, but his arm tightened around her waist. Kate couldn't have said if she leaned on him or if he picked her up or how, exactly, she got to the bench. All she could focus on was this man—with dark hair and dark eyes and tanned skin, wearing a motorcycle jacket over what looked like a pair of suit trousers. He sat her down on the bench and then took a seat next to her. "You're cold," he said, picking up her hand and rubbing it between his.

"Am I?" Yes, now that she thought about it, she could feel a chill in the air. The way he spoke to her called to mind someone trying to capture a bird with a broken wing.

Then something he'd said sank in. "You…you know Roger?"

The man—Seth? Had he said that was his name? Seth nodded. "I lived with him in college." He stood and peeled off his leather jacket and even though Kate was having a terrible day, she was struck by how nicely this strange, sympathetic man filled out a button-up shirt. He even had on a tie—but somehow, it didn't look stuffy. It looked dangerous, almost. "Frankly, I think you're doing the right thing," he went on as he settled his jacket around her shoulders. "Assuming he hasn't seen the light and become a better human, that is."

"No, I don't think he has," she said slowly. His

jacket was warm and soft, and she immediately felt a hundred times better. She had been cold for far too long. It was good to realize there could still be warmth in the world.

Then she realized what she'd said. "I didn't mean that," she quickly corrected, feeling the heat rise in her face. She blinked. Seth was staring at her with a level of focus that she wasn't used to. Roger certainly didn't listen to her like this.

But even thinking that made her feel terrible. She was supposed to be marrying Roger and she wasn't. She didn't have to add insult to injury by—well, by insulting him. "I mean, he's not a bad guy. He's a great catch." On paper.

On paper, Roger was handsome and educated, a successful small-business man. On paper he was perfect.

She couldn't marry a piece of paper.

She was supposed to be marrying a flesh-and-blood man who didn't love her. She was fairly certain about that.

"Even if he somehow magically turned into

a great catch—which I doubt," Seth said, fishing something out of his pants pockets and sitting next to her, "that doesn't mean he's a great catch for you."

Her breath caught in her throat as he closed the distance between them. As he lifted her chin and stared into her eyes, Kate knew she should pull away. She couldn't let this stranger kiss her. That wasn't who she was.

She was Kate Burroughs. Only child to Joe and Kathleen Burroughs. A real estate agent who worked for her parents at Burroughs Realty—which was now Burroughs and Caputo Realty.

She didn't make waves. She did the right thing, always. She got good grades and sold houses. She didn't get unexpectedly pregnant. She most definitely didn't leave her groom at the altar, and under no circumstances could she be attracted to a man who wasn't her fiancé.

At least, that was who she'd been yesterday. It seemed pretty obvious that she wasn't that same woman today.

He had such nice eyes. A deep brown, soft and

kind and yet still with an air of danger to him. He was dangerous to her, that much was clear, because he was going to kiss her and she was going let him and that was something the woman she'd been yesterday never would have allowed, much less entertained.

"It's going to be okay," he said softly. Then he touched her cheeks. With a handkerchief.

Kate hadn't realized she was crying until Seth dabbed at her cheeks.

When he was done, Seth pressed the handkerchief into her hand and leaned back. She wouldn't have thought it possible, but she got even more embarrassed. *Really, Kate? Really?* She wasn't even close to holding it together and she wanted to kiss this complete stranger?

She'd lost her mind. It was the only rational explanation.

She was relieved when Seth turned his gaze back out to the landscape. The sun was getting lower and the world was crimson and red. "Bolting on a wedding," he said slowly, "may not be cheap and it may not be easy. You may feel…"

"Like an idiot," she said bitterly.

"Confused," Seth corrected. "You're trying to talk yourself into going back, but your instincts made you leave. And it's a good idea to listen to your instincts."

"That's easy for you to say. Your parents didn't shell out thousands of dollars on a fairy-tale wedding and invite hundreds of guests, all of whom are probably wondering where the hell you are and what's wrong with you."

He made a huffing noise, as if she'd said something idiotic instead of stating the facts of the matter. "Correct me if I'm wrong, but your parents aren't marrying Roger. None of the guests are, either. You can put on a good show for them because of the sunk cost of the reception, but at the end of the day you're the one who has to go home with him. For the rest of your life." She shuddered involuntarily. Seth put his arm around her shoulders and, weak as she was, she leaned into his chest. He went on, "If he hasn't changed, then you don't want to be stuck with him."

She sniffed. She knew she was crying again,

but she was powerless to stop. Seth was warm and he smelled good and it was okay if she cried. "I don't. I really don't."

"Leaving him at the altar is cheaper and easier than getting a divorce," he said with finality. "Better to feel foolish now than to wake up tomorrow knowing you've made a huge mistake. Besides, if you realize you should have married him, you can still do that. If he really loves you, he'll understand."

That was what she needed to hear, because that was the truth that she felt in her heart. She was making a horrible mess for Roger and her parents, and she didn't want to humiliate him or their families and friends.

But at the end of the day, she was the one who had to live with him. With herself. And she *knew* she wouldn't be able to make the marriage last the rest of her life. How far would she and Roger get before she couldn't take it anymore? A year? Three? The divorce—because there would be one. Seth was right—would be ugly. Especially because of the baby.

She lost track of time, quietly crying into Seth's shoulder and his handkerchief as the sun got lower in the sky. Purple joined the reds and oranges. It was truly a beautiful late-summer day. Perfect for a wedding.

And where was she? Marrying her Prince Charming? Celebrating? No.

She was sitting on a bench with a man who had been Roger's roommate. A man who understood that Roger was better on paper than he was in real life.

A man who didn't think she was insane for running away from her own wedding.

"I'm pregnant," she announced because she hadn't been able to tell anyone yet and that single fact—those two little words—had completely altered the trajectory of her life.

Seth stiffened and then said, "Oh?" in a far too casual voice.

"Roger is the father," she went on in a rush of words. "I'm not the kind of person who would cheat on my fiancé." Ironically, though, she was the kind of person who'd abandon her fiancé.

What did that say about her? "It's his child and I should probably go back and marry him because we're going to have a baby. Together."

Seth didn't say anything, nor did he spring to his feet to lead her back to the limo. Back to her doom.

Wait—how did the limo get here? Had she stolen it?

And was it stealing if she'd rented it for the whole evening?

"Easy," Seth said again in that soothing voice of his. She could feel it in her chest, warm and comforting. "You might not believe this, but people have babies without being married all the time. It doesn't mean you've doomed your kid from the beginning."

"How can you say that?" And how was he reading her mind?

His arm tightened around her shoulders. "Because I've lived it, Kate. I won't let anything happen to you—I promise. Now," he went on even as she gasped at that honest promise—something she'd never heard cross Roger's lips, "do you remember where the limo came from?"

"Um…" She sat up and dabbed at her eyes again. The waterproof mascara was doing its best, but it was no match for this day and his handkerchief was paying the price. She tried to focus on the limo. "Stein, maybe?" It felt right— Stein Limo. That was a thing, she was pretty sure.

"Ron Stein? He's a great guy."

She stared at him in confusion. "You know the limo guy?" She didn't even know Seth's last name, but he knew Roger and now the limo guy. Was there anyone Seth didn't know?

"He rides," Seth said, as if that explained everything. "I'll see if I can make a call and let him know where his limo is. But I need you to stay right here, okay?"

"I don't know where you think I'd go. I'm not walking home." She wiggled her toes and realized she wasn't wearing her shoes. Where the hell were they?

But even the thought of going home made her

wince. She had a home—with Roger. They'd bought it last year, after finally setting a date for the wedding. It'd been a big sign of their commitment to each other.

No, that wasn't right. She didn't have a home with Roger. She owned part of a house. She shared a property with him. They split the bills right down the middle. They'd maintained separate bank accounts, even.

She'd lived with Roger, but it'd never felt like home.

"Promise me, Kate." His eyes were intense and serious. "You're not going anywhere without me."

"I promise." It wasn't like she'd sworn to love, honor or obey—but there was something to that promise that resonated in her mind.

Why could she make such a promise to this man she didn't know but couldn't to the one she did?

He gave her a satisfied nod of his head, leaned over and slid his hand inside his jacket, right over her left breast. She stiffened and he paused. "Just getting my phone," he said, purposefully not touching her. "Don't move." He stood and walked off to the side, far enough away that she couldn't hear what he was saying. But he turned back to her and gave her a little smile that set off butterflies in her stomach.

She ignored them and settled back on the bench, trying to get a handle on everything that happened.

It was a lot. But she'd had a good cry and Seth's jacket was warm and she felt better. Her mind was clearer and she could look past the next five minutes without having a panic attack.

She hoped.

She tried to rationally go over the facts. She was pregnant. She wasn't marrying Roger. She couldn't go back to the house she shared with him and she didn't think she could go to work on Monday. Her parents had sold half of Burroughs Realty to Roger in anticipation of the wedding. He owned it now.

She'd worked for Burroughs Realty her whole life, starting when they had her making copies and greeting clients as a little kid.

But they hadn't seen fit to give or even sell her part of the agency. Instead, they'd used it almost like a dowry, rewarding Roger for taking her off their hands.

Why hadn't she realized that before? She was a good real estate agent. She sold her market well. She was more than capable of being a full partner in the family business and running the office.

But it was Roger Caputo who was being rewarded with his name on the front door. Because why? Because he was marrying her?

She was their daughter. Wasn't she good enough on her own?

Oh, what would her parents say about all this? Especially once they found out she was pregnant? Her mother would try to be supportive—Kate hoped. The prospect of a grandbaby would be exciting, once the humiliation of a broken wedding passed.

But her father? Joe Burroughs was a dyed-in-the-wool workaholic who demanded perfection—or at the very least, that everything be done his way, and in his mind, those two things were the same.

She had to face the facts—her father might disown her for this, and if he did, he might forbid Mom from seeing Kate. Hadn't he already chosen Roger over her?

Just as she began to panic at the thought, Seth looked up at her again and smiled. It was a very nice smile, seemingly real and not the kind of expression one directed at a crazy person. He hadn't treated her like she was nuts at all, actually—even though the situation certainly did seem to warrant a little concern.

Instead of telling her she was insane to walk away from Roger, he'd agreed that tying herself to him was a bad idea. Anyone could have said the words, but Seth wasn't just saying them because she was having a really bad day. He was saying them because he actually *knew* Roger. Maybe not well, but he'd lived with Roger. He understood what that was like in a way that her friends and even her parents might not. Seth was speaking from a place of wisdom, and that counted for a lot.

It didn't make any sense that she felt safer with a strange man who rode a motorcycle than she did with the man she'd been with for four years, but there it was. Seth didn't know her at all, but he was more concerned with her well-being than anyone else. After all, how long had she been here? At least half an hour, maybe much longer. And had anyone come looking for her? Roger? Her parents? Any of the wedding guests?

No. Seth had stumbled upon her, noticed something was wrong, and he was actively making sure she was okay. He'd given her his leather jacket and dried her tears.

He glanced at her again, another smile on his lips—which set off another round of butterflies in her stomach. Now that her mind had cleared, it was hard to miss the fact that her Good Samaritan was also intensely handsome.

No, no—she was not going to be the kind of woman who defined herself by her attractions to men. It was blatantly obvious that she couldn't run from Roger's arms straight into a stranger's. She was pregnant, for God's sake. Romance should be the last thing on her mind.

She needed a place to stay tonight. Maybe tomorrow. She needed a job that didn't involve Roger or her father. She needed...

A plan. She couldn't sit here at a scenic overlook forever.

Had she managed to bring anything important with her—her wallet, money, credit cards, her license—*anything* that could help her out tonight? She rather doubted it—she didn't even know where her shoes were.

Seth ended his call and began to walk back toward her, and Kate realized something.

She needed him.

Three

"Come on," Seth said, pulling her to her feet. She was not a tiny thing—she was only a few inches shorter than he was—but there was still something delicate about her. "I'm going to take you to a hotel." Her eyes widened in surprise but she didn't lean away from him. Not that that mattered. "And I'm going to leave you there," he added with a smile.

"Oh. Of course," she said, her cheeks blushing a soft pink. "Thank you. I don't think I can go back to the house I shared with Roger." She cleared her throat. "Are we taking the limo?"

"No. I talked to Ron—he's going to send some-one out to pick it up. They did have cops look-ing for it but he's reported it not stolen. He's not going to press charges."

She blinked at him. "Is that because of you?"

The short answer was *yes*. Ron had been fu-rious that Kate had driven off with his limo—apparently it was his most expensive ride. He'd already fired the driver for dereliction of duties.

Ron's temper burned hot, but it always fizzled out quickly. Ron had been buddies with Billy Bolton for years and Seth had seen him in action plenty of times. He had to blow his top, and then he could be reasoned with.

Seth had waited until Ron finished blustering and then had convinced the man not to fire his driver—who had reasonably thought he'd had another hour before anyone would care about the whereabouts of the limo—and to inform the po-lice that no theft had been committed.

But that's not what he told her. Instead, Seth said, "Ron's a great guy. He understood." Kate notched an eyebrow at him—clearly she wasn't buying that line.

But that was his story and he was sticking to it. Kate had already had a terrible day. The prospect of being arrested and booked for grand theft auto would only make everything a thousand times worse and he didn't want that, especially now that she'd calmed down.

He hadn't lied when he'd told her he'd keep her safe. This pull he felt to protect her—from the consequences of taking a limo, from Roger, from her thoughtless parents, from the harsh realities of life as a single mother—it wasn't something that made sense on a rational level. He didn't know her. He had no claim to her.

But by God, he wasn't going to cast her to the winds of fate and call it a day.

"Okay," she finally said, exhaling heavily. Which did some very interesting things to her chest. "Then what do we do next?"

"We ride." The color drained out of her cheeks. "Have you ever been on a motorcycle before?"

She shook her head, her tilting hair bobbing

dangerously near her left ear. He reached up and tucked it back in place as best he could. He managed to do so without letting his fingers linger, so there was that.

"I've been riding for years," he assured her. "All you have to do is hold on. Can you do that?"

"I…" She looked down at her dress. "Um…"

She had a point. He eyed the confection suspiciously. The skirt was a full ball-gown style, layered with ruffles and lace. It spread out from Kate's waist in a circle that was easily five feet in diameter.

Ron had made it clear—Seth wasn't driving the limo. But Kate in that dress on the back of the chopper was a recipe for disaster. He could just imagine the wind getting underneath her skirts and blowing that dress up like a balloon.

"Is there any way to reduce the volume?" He tried to think back to what his aunt Stella had taught him about women's fashion. "An underskirt of some kind that we can remove?

Her face got redder. "I have on a structured petticoat. It's separate from the dress."

"Can you get it off?"

Kate's hands went to her waist. "I'm…I'm wearing a corset. I can't bend at the waist very well. And the skirt is tied on behind." She sounded unsure about the whole thing.

Seth mentally snorted to himself. Because if there was one thing a groom enjoyed on his wedding night, it was fighting through complicated layers of women's clothing. Petticoats and corsets—what was this, the 1800s? "How did you get into it?"

"I had help. My bridesmaids…"

Seth realized that if he wanted to get her on the bike anytime soon, he was going to have to play lady's maid. Which was not, he mentally reminded himself, the same as undressing her. At no point was he getting her naked.

No. Definitely not undressing a beautiful woman he wanted to pull into his arms and hold tight. Just…removing a few unnecessary layers of clothing. So that she could safely sit on his bike. That was all.

Trying to keep his mind focused on the task

at hand, he eyed the bodice of her dress. "Do you need to take the corset off?" he asked reluctantly, because that seemed less like removing layers and more like just stripping her completely bare.

She shook her head quickly. "I was able to drive in it, apparently. If we can get the petticoat off, it should be fine."

Of all the things Seth thought he'd be doing today, falling to his knees in front of a runaway bride and lifting the hem of her skirt over the voluminous petticoat was not something that had made the top ten. Or even the top one hundred. But that's what he was doing. He lifted the satin of her dress, rising as he moved the fabric up.

There should have been nothing sensual about this, lifting her skirts. She was still completely dressed. The petticoat stood between him and her body. God only knew how many layers were built into it, because she was still shaped like an inverted top. So this should have been nothing.

But there was something erotic about it.

Focus, Bolton, he scolded himself. This was

just an action born of necessity. He had to get her someplace safe, where people she knew could step up and take over. Taking care of a pregnant runaway bride was not in his skill set, and besides, it wasn't like he was attracted to her anyway.

Sure, she was beautiful—more so now that she'd calmed down. And yes, he was curious about what she looked like without the overdone hair, makeup and dress. And fine, he did feel a protective pull toward her. But that didn't add up to attraction any more than helping her adjust her outfit to ride on the bike was undressing her.

And that was final.

After a few snags—the petticoat was *huge*—he succeeded in getting the skirt up to her waist. He handed the bunched-up fabric to her and eyed the next layer. He could just see the bottom edge of her corset—white satin trimmed in baby blue. It appeared the waistband of the petticoat was underneath the corset.

This just kept getting better, because if he had to undo the corset, he'd have to remove the dress completely. He hoped it wouldn't come to that. If he were going to properly undress this woman, it sure as hell wouldn't be at a roadside pull-off.

He could see her chest rising and falling quickly. Did she feel the tension, too? Or was there something else?

He managed to pull his gaze away from her chest and found himself lost in her eyes. Her pupils were wide and dark and damn if she didn't look like a woman who was being undressed by a lover.

He put his hands on her waist, just below the bunched fabric of her skirt. Her waist felt right under his hands, warm and soft—and a little hard, thanks to the corset.

Who was he to talk about instincts? Yeah, she shouldn't get married when her instincts told her to run. But his were telling him to pull her against his chest and tuck her into his arms and not let go. And fighting that instinct only got harder when she lifted her gaze to his because she took his breath away.

"Turn around," he told her because he needed not to get lost in her eyes.

He needed to keep a cool head here—among other body parts. She was not for him. Only a complete asshole would take advantage of a woman in this situation. Seth was many things, but he didn't think he was an asshole, complete or otherwise.

She turned in his arms, and Seth forced himself to step back and assess the situation. Luckily, the corset didn't ride as low in the back as it did in the front. He could see where the petticoat was tied—in a knot.

Of course it was knotted.

He was tempted to just cut the damn thing off her body, but then a shiver raced over her skin. Brandishing a blade wasn't the best way to keep her calm, so Seth gritted his teeth and got on with it. It felt like it took forever, but after only a minute or so, the knot finally gave. "Now what?" he asked as the waistband sagged down around her hips.

She didn't answer for a moment. "I had to step

into it and they pulled it up because…" She swallowed. "Because it's so structured, it won't fall on its own. So I guess you'll have to push it down and I'll step out of it." Her voice shook.

Just for the ride, Seth repeated as he grabbed the waistband of the petticoat and worked it over her hips. *Structured* must mean *able to stand upright on its own*, because the damned fabric had no give in it at all. What kind of fresh hell was this, anyway?

The petticoat slipped over her skin, and he had to bite back his groan. He barely knew this woman and he wasn't even sure he liked her. But as he revealed the frilly lace of the white thong and the bare cheeks of her bottom, *liking* had nothing to do with it. His mouth went dry and his hands started to shake.

His instincts—they were pushing him past protective and into raw lust. He was strong, but how strong did one man have to be? Because he wasn't sure he could handle the way that thong left her bottom completely exposed.

Then it only got worse as he wrestled the petticoat down and revealed inch by creamy inch of her legs and bare skin. Why couldn't she be wearing those supportive bike shorts that some women wore instead of this scrap of lace? Why couldn't she be wearing a simpler outfit? Why couldn't she be someone who didn't inspire this reaction in him?

It only got worse when he hit the top of her thigh-high stockings and the blue garter on her right leg. Of course it matched the blue trim on her corset.

Roger, Seth concluded, was an idiot to let this woman go. Because Seth was pretty sure that he was going to have fantasies about this moment for the rest of his natural life.

He struggled not to touch her skin—but his hands shook even harder with the effort of it. Although he had to fight all that "structure" for every damned inch, he managed to get the petticoat pushed down to the ground, which meant that he was at eye level with her bottom. And it was perhaps one of the nicer bottoms he had ever seen. Firm and rounded and begging to be touched.

Except it wasn't. This was not a seduction. This was an action born of necessity. He would not touch her. She'd already had a bad day, and being groped by a biker wouldn't make anything better.

"Now what?" His voice cracked with the strain of trying to sound normal. "Do you just step out?" That was when he realized she didn't have on shoes. They were standing on gravel. Had she been missing her shoes the entire time?

"I…I don't want to lose my balance," she said in a strangled-sounding voice. Before Seth could process what she meant by that, she turned. Which was good due to the fact that he was no longer staring at her ass.

But now he was staring at her front. The thin lace of her virginal white thong covered the vee of her sex and everything about Seth came to a screeching halt. His blood, his breath—nothing worked. He couldn't even blink as he stared at her body.

It only got worse when she placed one hand on

his shoulder for balance. Seth squeezed his eyes shut because there was no point in looking if he couldn't have her, and he *couldn't* have her. Offering anything beyond assistance would be a mistake. She'd run away from a wedding today. She was pregnant with another man's baby. None of her was for him.

Even though his eyes were closed, the scent of her body surrounded him, torturing him. It wasn't the scent of arousal, but there was no missing the sweet notes of flowers—maybe lilacs, and a hint of vanilla that had been buried underneath the layers. Her smell reached out and stroked him, making him shake with need.

She stepped out of the petticoat and—thankfully—let go of the skirt. It fell, covering her legs and hiding that lacy thong and those white thigh-highs and that garter belt from his eyes. Seth gave himself another few moments to make sure he had himself under control.

Then she let out a little cry and stumbled. He moved without thinking, catching her before she fell. His arms folded around her body and finally, he was able to pull him to her.

But despite his awareness of her body—and the fact that her arms went around his neck so that he could feel her breasts pressing against his chest—he didn't miss the way she shivered or how her breathing was ragged.

"Easy," he said, coming to his feet with her in his arms.

"I stepped on a rock," she said, her voice wavering. She sounded like she was on the verge of tears again, and that hurt him in a way he hadn't expected.

He wanted to make sure she didn't hurt. He'd wanted that from the very beginning. But now, it felt more personal.

He didn't understand this strange drive to take care of her. He could've called her a ride. Surely someone could've come to get her. Rapid City had taxis, and for a price they could've made it out this far.

But he hadn't. He hadn't done anything except hold her close and make sure she was okay.

He didn't want to think too much about why.

He carried her over to his bike and sat her on the back. He gave thanks that his father had built this prototype with the passenger seat behind the driver's seat. Part of Billy Bolton's rigorous testing was to make sure that he took Seth's mom, Jenny, out for rides with him. Billy claimed that sometimes, the additional weight of a passenger would reveal design flaws that needed to be tweaked. Because Seth didn't want to consider any other options about what happened when his parents went out riding, he accepted that explanation at face value.

"I'll put the petticoat in the car and then we'll go, okay?" he said. "But you're going to have to straddle the bike. See if you can figure that out with your skirts." He waved a hand over her dress and hoped like hell he wouldn't have to take the whole thing off to get her corset removed.

But even as he thought that, his brain decided it would be a really great idea. He would kill to see Kate Burroughs in nothing but a corset and some stockings and a garter. Splayed out on the bed, a package that Seth was almost done un-wrapping.

He slammed the brakes on that line of thought. *Nope.* She had too many bags to carry, and he was a single twenty-five-year-old man. He had no interest in tangling with someone whose personal life was as messy as Kate Burroughs's was. No matter how good she looked, no matter how sweet she smelled, no matter how much she'd clung to his neck.

No matter how right she'd felt in his arms.

She nodded and he went back to get the petticoat. It was all dirty with rocks and bits of grass stuck in it. He shoved it into the back of the limo and glanced around, hoping against hope that there would be a purse with a wallet, but nothing. There was some champagne that was probably warm, though. But he didn't think that'd help anything right now.

He locked the limo and left the keys on the ground on the inside of the front driver's-side wheel, where Stein had told him to leave them. True dark was settling now and it was going to be a long, cold ride back to Rapid City. It wouldn't be so bad if he had his jacket, but he couldn't let her freeze to death behind him.

The other logistical problem was that he only had one helmet. He had no idea if it would fit over her hair.

He went back to the bike and picked up the helmet. "Let's see if this works," he said. At the very least, she had managed to straddle the bike. The skirt had hiked up over her calves, and her legs were going to be cold by the time they got out of the hills, but there was no way he could risk having her fall off if she was riding sidesaddle. Maybe if she pressed herself against him, his body could take the worst of the wind. He'd be a Popsicle by the time they made town, but he'd take it for her.

But even that noble sentiment was almost completely overridden by the image of her arms around his waist, her chest pressed to his back, her legs tucked behind his. Of that lacy little thong and the corset.

Of a wedding night that ended differently.

He pulled at the collar of his shirt. Yeah, maybe he wouldn't freeze.

She looked up at him, her eyes wide. "I can't thank you enough, Seth," she said, her voice soft. "I'm having a really bad day, but you're making it better."

If she were anyone else, he'd cup her cheek and stroke her skin with his thumb. He'd tilt her head back and brush his lips over hers. He'd offer comfort in a completely different way.

But she wasn't anyone else. She was Roger's pregnant runaway bride. So instead of kissing her, he settled the helmet over her hair. It didn't work. He pulled it off. "Let me see what I can do here." She tilted her head so he could get at the elaborate updo—it probably had some sort of name, but he didn't have any idea about women's hair. He could see the pins and clips—sparkly stuff in her hair. And hairspray. Lots of hairspray. He began pulling them out and shoving them into his pants pocket. What would her hair feel like without all this crap in it? Soft and silky—the kind of hair he could bury his hands in.

He really had to get a grip. The whole mass of hair sagged and then fell. It looked awkward and painful, but he was sure he could fit the helmet on now. "There."

She looked back at him as he settled the helmet on her head and strapped it under her chin. She looked worried. "This will be fun," he promised. Cold, but fun. "Just hold on to me, okay?"

She nodded. Seth took his seat and fired up the engine. It rumbled beneath him. He loved this part of riding. Bringing the machine to life and knowing that a journey was ahead of him.

After a moment's hesitation, Kate's arms came around his waist. His brain chose that exact moment to wonder—when was the last time he'd had a woman on the back of a motorcycle?

Of course he'd ridden with women before. That was one of the reasons to ride a bike—women loved a bad boy, and Seth was more than happy to help them act out their fantasies. Motorcycles were good seduction and he was a red-blooded American man. He wasn't above doing a little seducing.

But there was something different about this—about Kate. This wasn't a seduction, leaving aside the fact that he knew what her thong looked like. This was something else, and he couldn't put a name to it.

Then he felt more than heard her sigh against the back of his neck as the helmet banged his shoulder. He winced but didn't flinch as she settled her cheek against his back, her arms tightening around him even more. Her body relaxed into his. Which was good. Great. Wonderful. The tighter she held on, the safer this ride would be.

Except his body was anything but relaxed. He was rock hard and she'd know it if her grip slipped south in any way.

He needed to get her to a hotel and then he needed to get on his way. He had a future as a partner of Crazy Horse Choppers. He had plans for the business. He had motorcycles to sell.

None of those things involved a pregnant runaway bride.

He rolled away from the scenic overlook and hit the road back to Rapid City.

Kate Burroughs wasn't in his plans. After today, he wasn't going to see her or her stockings ever again.

That was final.

Four

"Good morning, Katie," Harold Zanger said, strolling into Zanger Realty with a smile on his face and a bow tie around his neck. "It's a zinger of a day at Zanger, isn't it?"

As cheesy as the line was—and it had been cheesy every single day for the last month and a half—Kate still smiled. She smiled every day now. "It is indeed, Harold," she said.

Harold Zanger was one of her father's oldest friends. They'd been playing poker together for a good forty years—longer than Kate had been alive. Harold was almost an uncle to her.

Kate had not gone back to Burroughs and Caputo Realty. She just couldn't—especially when her parents had made it clear that splitting Roger off from the business was going to be quite complicated, which was one way to say that her father wasn't going to do it because he was beyond furious with her.

So it had been Kate to decide that, rather than grovel before her father and Roger, she'd start over. She was the one who put distance between them.

It had hurt more than she wanted it to, to be honest. Although she'd known it wasn't likely, she'd wanted her parents to put her first. She'd wanted them to take her side and tell her it'd all work out. She'd wanted her mom to get excited about the pregnancy.

She'd wanted the impossible. Oh, Mom was excited—to the extent that she'd underlined the word *excited* three times in the congratulations card she'd sent. Other than that, there'd been no discussion of pregnancies, no trips down memory lane, no planning for the baby's room.

There hadn't been anything, really, since Kate had walked out of their house and driven back to the hotel where she'd been staying since Seth had dropped her off and paid for three nights.

And the hell of it was, it wasn't like they had put Roger first. No, Joe and Kathleen Burroughs had done what they always did—they'd put their business first. Burroughs Realty—Burroughs and Caputo Realty now—had always been the most important thing. Her father hadn't disowned her outright, but it was clear that, for the time being, there was no point in pursuing a family relationship. Joe Burroughs was a workaholic and Kathleen refused to go against her husband's wishes.

No, the business came first, and Roger was now part owner of the business, which meant that Roger came first. So Kate had left because she hadn't wanted to make things difficult for her mother.

Harold Zanger, gregarious and happy, had offered her a job. Kate strongly suspected it had put a strain on his friendship with Joe Burroughs, but

Harold insisted everything was fine. Of course, he was an eternal optimist, so perhaps everything was. Harold had given her a desk and a blazer and some business cards and told her to "get out there and sell some houses, sweetheart."

If anyone else had called Kate *sweetheart*, she would've walked, but Harold had been calling her sweetheart since she was old enough to crawl— probably even before that.

So here she was. Ready to get out there and sell some houses for Zanger Realty.

"Today's the day," Harold said, snapping the suspenders underneath his Zanger Realty blazer, which was a delightful shade of goldenrod. "Something big is going to happen today, Katie my girl. I can feel it."

There was comfort in familiarity and Harold said this to her every morning. She hadn't be-lieved it at first—she still didn't really believe it—but Harold's optimism was infectious.

"Today's the day," she agreed.

"Your big sale," Harold all but crowed, "is going to walk through that door. I just know it."

"I'm sure it will," she said with an indulgent smile. Really, it was sweet that Harold believed what he said, because that was just the kind of man he was and had always been. If opposites attract, then that held true for friendships, too. Joe Burroughs had been a pessimist, convinced that tomorrow the bottom would fall out and the world would end and so he'd better sell a house today so that his family would have something to live on. Disaster was always lurking right around the corner for Joe Burroughs, so he had to miss his daughter's concerts and plays because there was work to be done.

Harold was the opposite. Today was a good day. Tomorrow would be even better. It would all work out in Harold's world, and Kate would be lying to herself if she said she didn't need that in her life right now.

Because she was three months pregnant. She'd sold exactly two houses—but they hadn't been big sales. She'd earned enough on commission to rent a two-bedroom apartment and buy some secondhand furniture. But she had to sell a lot of houses in the next six months if she wanted to be able to take time off when she had her baby.

Roger would pay child support. Just because he didn't love her and she didn't love him didn't mean that he would leave her out to dry. Roger wasn't a bad guy, really.

But when they had sat down face-to-face and confronted the aftermath of their relationship and the baby that would always tie them together, it had been clear—he'd been relieved that she'd walked away. And he hadn't even tried to hide it. He'd gone on their honeymoon trip to Hawaii without her and he hadn't missed her at all.

Even more than that, Roger had been relieved when her father had not asked him to give up his stake in the real estate business. Which really had Kate wondering—had he been marrying her be-cause of her or for the business?

She knew the answer—the business—but she couldn't think about that.

If she ever had another wedding, she would be damned sure she was marrying someone who wanted her. Not her family's business. Not her name.

Her. Kate Burroughs. Future single mom and semiprofessional hot mess.

Aside from child support, Roger made something else clear—they were done. He wasn't going to be an active part of raising his child. It was painful, it really was. But at the same time, it was also a relief. She wouldn't have to worry about navigating around Roger at the same school plays and concerts that her own father had skipped. She wouldn't have to negotiate who would get the baby for Christmas and birthdays. It would be simpler without Roger.

It would be harder—she was under no illusions that being the single mother of a newborn wouldn't be the hardest thing she'd ever done. But she only had to negotiate with herself.

She was on her own. For the first time in her life, she didn't have to answer to anyone. Not her father, not Roger, not her mother. There was something freeing about that. Terrifying, but freeing.

Harold went back to his office and Kate turned to her listings. She had been a real estate agent for years, so it wasn't like she was learning on the job. She knew what to do. She had grown up at Burroughs Realty, copying things for her parents and then going with them when they looked at houses. She'd learned how to stage a house when she was in high school. Her parents had paid her for her help, although not a lot.

She could sell a home in her sleep. But she needed buyers and sellers. She needed someone to walk through that door and instead of asking for Harold, to ask for Kate. That was what she'd had at Burroughs Realty. She had been a Burroughs, and any Burroughs would do for some people. The name was the important thing.

As her thoughts often did when she was faced with the weight of her future, she imagined that one person in particular walking through the door—a tall, dark, mysterious biker. A man who looked dangerous and yet treated her as if she were worth protecting.

Seth Bolton.

She had not seen him since he had taken her to a local hotel and shaken her hand in the lobby. He hadn't even suggested that he come up to the room and make sure she got settled. He was too good a guy for that.

That had to be why she couldn't stop thinking about him. It had felt like…like there was unfinished business between them. Which was ridiculous. They didn't have any business together to begin with. She'd had the worst day of her life and he'd taken pity on her. That was all there was—a Good Samaritan doing a kind deed for a woman having a really terrible day. Because there was no way a man like that was single or available. And even if he were—why would he be interested in her? She had not made the best of first impressions.

Looking back at what had happened over six weeks ago, she could see with a little objective distance that she had been in a state of complete and total shock. Discovering she was pregnant had left her stunned. Deciding she couldn't marry Roger had been a realization that sent her reeling. Each shock mounted upon the next. She still didn't remember stealing the limo, but at least she hadn't been arrested. Whatever Seth had done or said to the limo owner had worked. The cops hadn't gotten involved, and she was beyond grateful for that. He had helped her see that her reasons for running were valid, made sure she was okay and let her cry it out.

But gratitude wasn't the only reason she kept thinking about him. There'd been the way he'd untied her petticoat and slid it down her legs. And the way she'd wrapped her arms around his waist and leaned into him on the long, cold ride back to Rapid City. Hell, even just the way his jacket had smelled—leather and something lighter, maybe sandalwood. He'd smelled good.

She was not fantasizing about the man. Oh, sure, he drifted through her dreams every so often, but that didn't mean she was fantasizing about him, specifically.

It was the fact that he had taken care of her. And she had needed to be taken care of. That was all.

She didn't need to be coddled anymore. She'd gotten back on her feet. Her parents and Roger had handled the entire disaster with a surprising amount of good humor—for them, anyway. But that didn't change the fact that, moving forward, she needed to sell a house. A lot of houses. Heck, even one big sale would get her through the winter.

While she was wishing for the impossible, she might as well ask for a pony. Sadly, Santa had never delivered on that one, either.

As she mused, she worked on assembling a potential list of houses. A family from out of town had called and said that the husband might be relocating to Rapid City. Nothing was definite yet, but there was a good chance that they'd move and if so, Kate was going to be the one to sell them a house. Harold had gifted her with this opportunity, rather than keep it for himself.

The Murray family had given her their standard list of requirements—three bedrooms, two baths, a fenced backyard, a two-car garage. She was putting together a list of potential homes and praying that Mr. Murray decided to take a job in Rapid City when the door jingled.

On reflex, Kate said, "It's a zinger of a day at Zanger. Can I help you?"

Then she looked up at the same moment a hearty chuckle reached her ears. There was something familiar about that chuckle, warm and comforting.

She froze. There was something familiar about the man standing in the entryway. Tall, dark. Black hair, dark eyes—that motorcycle jacket settled over his shoulders like a second skin.

And that smile. She didn't remember everything from her wedding day. But that smile? She'd been dreaming about that smile for a month. She was helpless to *stop* dreaming about it.

It was entirely possible, she decided as she stared at him, that she was still asleep because her fantasy had just walked into her office and into her life, hotter than ever. This was the man who'd talked her off the ledge. Who'd supported her when she'd admitted that marrying Roger would've been the biggest mistake of her life.

Who'd practically stripped her bare at a road-side overlook.

"Kate," he said, his voice stroking over her name in a way that made her toes curl. "I was hoping I'd find you."

Okay, that did it. She was definitely dreaming. "Seth? What are you doing here?"

If she were dreaming, the answer would be *I have come to sweep you off your feet, my darling. Let me take you away from all of this and solve all your problems.*

"I looked you up."

She blinked. "You did? Why?"

"I wanted to see how you were doing." He took another step into the office. "How are you doing?"

Her breath caught in her throat. As odd as it seemed, not many people asked that question. The fallout from leaving Roger at the altar had shown her who her true friends were—and the number was few and far between. Really, her mother was the only one who asked that question and was actually interested in the answer.

Except for Seth Bolton, a stranger who had seen her at her lowest moment. Instead of running, he'd stood by her side. He'd taken care of her. He'd made everything better.

Was it any wonder she'd been dreaming of him nearly every night?

This wasn't possible. She could not be watching Seth walk into her office, that sexy smile on his face, asking about how she was. It simply wasn't possible.

"I…I'm fine," she told him. "I mean, I'm all right."

"Good." His smile deepened and she was stunned to realize that he had dimples. What a difference. That made him hot and sweet and more than everything she dreamed of. "I meant to check in on you earlier, but I had some business to deal with first."

She lifted her eyebrows at that. Was he serious? She was nothing to him, other than a strange afternoon that had probably become an amusing anecdote. *Did I ever tell you about the time*

I found a runaway bride in the middle of the Black Hills?

She would expect that if he remembered her at all, he'd remember the crazy woman who stole a limo and refused to marry the father of her child. Nobody should've found her desirable. Memorable, maybe. Definitely not someone worth worrying about.

"Well, as you can see, everything's okay." That was a gross generalization. She was exhausted and hormonal and worried sick about how she was going to make everything work out.

But she wasn't the same lost woman he'd found by the side of the road, either. She held her head high and faced every challenge she met with open eyes. She had a job and a purpose. She didn't need to be coddled anymore.

Not even by someone as attractive as Seth Bolton. Was it possible that he was even more gorgeous now? He took another step closer and she swore she could feel the tension between them hum, like he'd plucked the string of a violin.

The jacket was the same, but he had on a gray

T-shirt with some sort of logo on it and a pair of well-worn jeans that were black. They hung low on his hips and she realized she was staring at the vee of his waist as if she'd never noticed that part of a man before.

She jerked her gaze back up, her cheeks hot. His lips quirked into a smile that did things to her. Things she hadn't felt in over a month.

No, she scolded herself. It was one thing to fantasize about a great guy she'd never have to face again. It was a completely different affair to lust after a flesh-and-blood man standing in a real estate office.

Why was he standing in a real estate office? She cleared her throat and tried to relocate her lost sense of professionalism. "Was there something I could help you with?" Or had he just come here to make sure she hadn't completely fallen apart? She hoped not. She didn't want him to think of her as this pitiful creature who couldn't function.

That string of tension that had been humming between them tightened as his eyes darkened.

His gaze swept over her face, her body. Was he checking her out? Or just checking for signs of her pregnancy? It was still pretty early. Her clothes still mostly fit, although she'd already gone up a cup size in bras.

"Actually, there is," he said. "As crazy as it sounds, I'm settling down."

Oh. That sounded like…like he was setting up house with a girlfriend. Or a wife. Well. So much for that fantasy. She was not about to poach anyone's man. At least now he'd stay safely in her dreams and she wouldn't make a fool of herself over him.

She stood from the desk, straightening her tacky Zanger jacket. "I can handle all your needs. Your *real estate* needs," she added, her face burning.

Well. So much for not making a fool of herself over him.

For a second, she wished she were someone different—someone more together and charming and…

Well, someone who wasn't pregnant and coming out of a long-term relationship.

He didn't laugh. Or even snort. Instead, something in his eyes changed—deepened—and warmth spread through her body. She recognized that warmth—*desire*. It was like running into an old friend from high school she hadn't seen in a few years. She hadn't realized how much she'd missed it—until here it was.

When was the last time she had felt desire? At one point she was sure she had enjoyed sleeping with Roger, but she couldn't remember when it stopped being fun and started being routine. It hadn't been bad. It just hadn't been good.

Kind of like Roger himself.

Seth was still smiling. It would be great if she could get her act together today. Within the hour, even though that was probably too much to ask.

Still, she had to give it a try. "What sort of properties are you looking for? Because a home is very different from a condo." There. That was a viable thing to say that didn't make her sound like an idiot.

And if she wasn't making any sense, she was blaming that on the pregnancy, which went right back to Roger. So if she was flabbergasted before Seth for the second time in a few short weeks, it would be entirely Roger's fault.

She motioned for Seth to sit because standing was getting more awkward by the second. Seth took the chair in front of her desk and crossed one of his legs, bringing his heavy leather boots into view. Up closer, Kate could see that the T-shirt was for Crazy Horse Choppers, which fit with the leather jacket and the motorcycle.

In other words, he looked like a badass biker dude.

Except for those dangerous dimples. Because it took everything hard about him and made it something else. Something that had her pulse pounding in her veins, heating her from the inside out. "Tell me what you're looking for."

He held her gaze for a beat too long before he spoke. "Well, I've been back in Rapid City for about a month and a half."

Wait—did that mean he'd been living somewhere else until…until when? Had he come back for the wedding that wasn't? "Where were you before?"

"I'm not sure if you recognize my name or not but my family owns Crazy Horse Choppers."

"Um…no? I'm sorry," she quickly added. "I mean, of course I've heard of Crazy Horse Choppers."

They were one of Rapid City's most famous local businesses, started twenty or thirty years ago by a local boy made good and now run by his three sons, whose names hadn't ever really registered for Kate. She thought there'd been a reality show featuring the three unruly biker brothers a number of years ago. Kate had been in high school when it'd been on the air—and it hadn't been interesting to her then.

Clearly, she'd underestimated the power of a bad boy in a leather jacket.

She shook her head, trying to push that thought away. She was definitely going to blame that line of thinking on the pregnancy hormones. "I just didn't make the connection between you and the company," she explained. "I'm not up-to-date on motorcycles. I'd never even been on one until…"

Until he'd stripped her petticoat off her and set her on the back of his bike and she'd wrapped her arms around his waist and held on to him.

She wouldn't have thought it possible, but her face got even hotter.

"I lived in LA for a year while managing the Crazy Horse showroom we operate there," Seth said, ignoring her red face. "My father and my uncles recently made me partner in the company, so I'm thinking I need to set up a permanent base."

She eyed him. She had no idea how old Seth was, but he seemed young to be a partner in such a successful company. Was that just because it was the family business and he was family? Or was he really good at what he did?

Of course it was because he was good at what he did. He'd talked her down from the ledge, hadn't he? The man could probably sell motorcycles to anyone.

"'Permanent base'? That's not how most people describe buying a house." In fact, it sounded more like he was setting up a strategic military outpost or something.

He shrugged. "My uncle Bobby has wild expansion plans. He expects me to travel and represent the brand. But the company is based here, so I need to maintain a residence. I anticipate that I'll only be in Rapid City maybe half the year. The other thing—"

"The other thing?" A house would be a great sale. As partner to a successful and growing business, he'd want something that spoke of his power and, one assumed, wealth. Or at the very least, a condo with all the bells and whistles.

"I'm in the planning phase for a new project for Crazy Horse," he went on, ignoring her interruption. "We're going to need an industrial space for a museum."

Her mouth fell open. A house was terrific. A house *and* an industrial space?

She'd be able to live off that commission for months. She could take time off to be with her baby without having to worry about money.

Seth Bolton was her guardian angel. It was really that simple.

He was staring at her expectantly. "Kate? You okay?"

"What? Oh. Yes. Yes! I'm just…a museum?"

That grin made it plenty clear that she wasn't fooling him. "My granddad and my dad have been building choppers for thirty years. My dad's kept one of everything he's ever built, including a lot of prototypes that never saw production. He's got close to four hundred motorcycles stored in the original Crazy Horse factory. I think we can build the brand loyalty if we take those bikes out of storage and put them on display. Harley-Davidson did something similar and they've had a great response."

"Wow…" she said, which was lame and stupid but really, how was she supposed to react here? Seth Bolton was hot, kind, supportive…hot—and now also an amazing salesman and a whip-smart business owner?

Her fantasies weren't this good. They just weren't. If he also loved babies and puppies and was single, then she'd know for certain that she was having the best dream of her life.

Nothing about this made the least bit of sense. Not only was the man of her dreams—literally—sitting in front of her, suddenly in the market for a great deal of real estate, the commissions of which could carry her through the next several months, but he was part of Rapid City's most famous local family.

Underneath the desk, she pinched her leg. But nothing changed. Seth was still sitting in front of her, dimples in full force, ready to discuss all his real estate needs while also giving her those searing looks.

She was in trouble. The very best kind of trouble.

Five

One thing was clear, Seth realized as he sat across from Kate while she called up listings to give him an idea of what was on the market.

He should have checked on her sooner.

He remembered a hot woman. Okay, that had been more her body than her face because she'd had a very bad day and had looked like hell. But it was hard to forget skimming that petticoat down her legs, revealing her gorgeous ass in that little scrap of fabric—not to mention the stockings and garter.

He shifted in his seat. The woman sitting across

from him in a tacky yellow blazer with Zanger embroidered on the chest wasn't *hot*.

Kate Burroughs was beautiful.

Without the false eyelashes and lopsided hair—and without the lost look in her eyes—Kate was simply stunning. Even more so because today, while it was clear that she was shocked to see him, she wasn't in a state of shock. And what a difference that made.

He might be imagining things, but she even seemed happy to see him. Surprised, sure. Excited about the business he was throwing her way, yes. But Seth saw the way she looked at him—especially the way her whole face had softened when he'd asked how she was doing.

He should've come sooner. But he'd had to represent Crazy Horse Choppers at two trade shows and Julie's soccer season had started, and although it wasn't good for his image as a tough biker, Seth was the kind of guy who went to his baby sister's games and cheered her on from the sidelines. Then there'd been a powwow on the reservation and career day at the school where his mom taught and moving out of his folks' house into the hotel and putting his stuff in storage and…life happened.

But he hadn't forgotten Kate Burroughs. That wasn't possible, not after their memorable introduction. But it wasn't until he'd come to the belated realization that at the age of twenty-five, he couldn't continue to live in a hotel that he had decided to seek her out.

It'd taken a lot of digging. She had apparently been the Burroughs in Burroughs and Caputo Realty for some years. Seth wasn't entirely sure what the deal was, since she was now at Zanger Realty and Roger was still at Burroughs and Caputo Realty. The whole situation was messy and Seth was not interested in messy.

Which did not explain why he was currently sitting across from the messiest woman he'd ever met.

That wasn't fair, though. She'd been a mess the day of her failed wedding, yeah. But the woman before him now? If he hadn't known she was pregnant, he never would've guessed. She looked amazing. Her golden-brown hair was free of the shellacked mass of curls that had overwhelmed her delicate features. Her hair was away from her face, but the rest of it fell in gentle waves down her back. Her eyes were the same startlingly bright green he remembered and today, they were clear and hopeful instead of lost and afraid. Without the heavy layer of makeup, he felt like he was seeing her for the first time.

Seth had seen a lot of attractive women in his time. Los Angeles was overflowing with them. But that was hotness for public display and public consumption.

Kate was more of a quiet beauty. There was just something about her.

Which was the only possible explanation as to why he was here. He couldn't stop thinking about that something and it went way beyond thongs and garter belts.

"So if you'll be traveling a lot, a condo would probably be the best property for you. The exterior maintenance is…" Seth scowled at her.

Anyone else would have been terrified. But Kate merely lifted her eyebrows and…smiled? "No?"

"Don't condos—by definition—have other people living in close proximity?"

She tilted her head to one side, studying him. "Yes. It's not a stand-alone building. You would have neighbors with whom you'd share walls."

He shook his head. "No. LA was full of people who talked all the time because they were afraid if they didn't, no one would notice how important they were. I couldn't stand it." Among other things. He'd hoped that getting the hell out of South Dakota would be the answer for this restlessness.

It hadn't been. Traveling the world and selling motorcycles was probably the cure for what ailed him.

Yet here he was, buying a damned house while planning on barely living in it. He went on, "I want peace and quiet. No neighbors."

"You're talking to me," she pointed out, pinning him to his chair with her gaze.

"You're different," he said and the funny thing

was, it wasn't a line he was feeding her. He meant it. He couldn't have said why, but she was. "So I need a house."

"With enough land to protect you from nosy neighbors. What else do you need? I'm assuming a garage is important—or room to build your own?"

He had to hand it to her as she grilled him on the number of bathrooms and bedrooms he required or if he wanted a finished basement or would he consider building from scratch—the woman knew what she was doing. He'd had some vague notion of a house that he now realized didn't look all that different from his parents' home.

But his parents' home was built for a family. And Billy's bikes, but it'd been sprawling enough to house the fourteen-year-old boy Seth had been when Billy had married Jenny Wawausuck and adopted Seth and big enough to hold them all when Julie had been born the next year.

It'd been a family home. And that was not what Seth wanted, as he had no plans to start a family anytime soon. Not even by accident. He was careful.

So he wasn't settling down. Not even a possibility. Billy Bolton—hell, all the Bolton men—might be dyed-in-the-wool family men, but Seth was a Bolton in name only.

Still, he needed a place to keep his stuff and the freedom to come and go—and have guests over—without his parents keeping tabs on him.

He looked at the photos of the four or five houses she'd pulled up, but nothing jumped out at him. "I need to walk through them," he said.

"Absolutely," she agreed. "Pictures can tell us a lot, but they can't give you a real sense of how the house will work for you. I'll need to schedule tours, if that's all right. Only a few of these houses are empty. Unless you are looking to buy today?"

Seth snorted. "This isn't a snap decision. I want to make sure I find the right place. Even if I don't live there full-time, I still want it to be home." He didn't know if that was possible or not, but at the very least, he wanted something he could be proud of.

Besides, owning and caring for his own home would just further prove to his father and his uncles that they'd made the right decision in making Seth a partner in Crazy Horse Choppers, and he couldn't let the Bolton men down. Not after everything they'd done for him.

His parents hadn't been huge fans of Seth relocating to a hotel and, aside from room service, neither was Seth. But as much as he loved his family, he hadn't been able to move back in with them after a year in LA. So if he had to pay for a hotel, then he paid for the hotel. He had the money to spare.

Kate nodded eagerly. "And if none of these houses are right, there are always more houses coming on the market. Sometimes we get notice before properties are officially listed—as long as you've got the time, the right house for you is out there."

She made it sound like it was only a matter of patience. Seth was not always the most patient of people. His dad said it was because he was still young and stupid—although Seth didn't feel particularly young or particularly stupid.

Seth was afraid it was something else. Billy was a good father—but it wasn't his blood that ran through Seth's veins. What if this restlessness wasn't just youth?

What if it was something he'd inherited from his birth father, the sperm donor?

Seth pushed that question away. He didn't like to compare himself to the man who'd abandoned Jenny Wawausuck when she'd been pregnant, never to show his face again. Seth was a Bolton now. The past didn't matter. Only the future.

A future where he owned a sizable chunk of a family business as well as his own home. "That's fine. Saturday? We can make a day of it. Unless you have other plans?"

Because he had no idea. It was a fair assumption that, since she was no longer at the office where Roger worked and—he glanced down at her hand—she wasn't wearing any ring, she wasn't actively involved with anyone. Kate didn't strike him as the kind who rebounded indiscriminately.

But that didn't mean she might not have something to do on a Saturday.

Kate smiled and damn if Seth wasn't dazzled by it. "Saturday would be perfect. Now tell me about this museum you're planning. Does it need to be close to the production facility? Do you want to build to suit or adapt a preexisting space? Do you have a handle on how much square footage you're looking at?"

Seth took a deep breath. The museum was his idea—he'd toured the Harley-Davidson museum in Milwaukee a while back and had been damned impressed. He didn't want to replicate that facility, because the Crazy Horse collection was vastly different from the Harley collection.

Seth still remembered the first time Billy had taken him to see all the choppers that he'd built. Seth had been like a kid in a candy store. The original choppers were impressive, but what had blown his teenaged mind had been the wild prototypes Billy had created over the years.

That was what he wanted to capture—that feeling of shock and awe that only a Crazy Horse chopper could inspire. And he wanted to capitalize on that experience. The motorcycle business had its ups and downs and having a secondary stream of income—or even tertiary stream—to help even out the lows was a good business decision. After several interesting discussions—and only one fistfight—the Boltons had agreed to spot him the capital. He just needed a property.

Besides, it wasn't like he was making it up as he went along. He had a master's in business administration. He hadn't needed a college degree to build choppers—he'd been doing that by Billy's side since he'd been thirteen.

But running a business was not the same thing as welding a frame. And the Bolton men had been good to Seth for last ten years of his life. His father and his uncles were demonstrating a great deal of faith in Seth. He couldn't screw this up and run the family legacy into the ground. His adopted last name meant he had to make sure the family business stayed relevant and important.

"We're still in the idea phase," he finally said. Which really meant it was all still in his head. "At least sixty thousand square feet. I'm envisioning the museum, a gift store, a café—maybe an area where we can have special exhibits. And possibly a showroom. We're still selling bikes out of the factory, but I don't think that's sustainable. If it's closer to the original factory, that'd be ideal, but it doesn't have to be. I hope that makes sense," he added.

Her eyes lit up. He couldn't tell if she was excited by the vision or the commission it would generate. Which was fine. He didn't need her to be excited about his big plans. Once he'd realized she was in real estate, the whole reason he'd come looking for her at work was to give her the commission. It'd been important to him.

He honestly wasn't sure why—she wasn't his responsibility. But he needed several properties, and he wasn't on a first-name basis with any other real estate agents. So why shouldn't he help out a soon-to-be single mom? God knew that Seth's mom could've used a hand up before Billy came into their lives.

He was paying forward the good fortune Billy Bolton had brought into Seth's life. It was that simple.

But it didn't feel simple when Kate leaned forward, her gaze locked on his. It felt messy and complicated and...right.

"It makes perfect sense," she told him. "But I'm going to need to do some research as to what's available. Do you have a budget in mind?"

Seth shifted nervously. The budget was, predictably, the part Ben and Billy objected to the most. "I'd like to get a list of potential properties and the associated costs first so we can budget for design and building after that." Billy was not in the mood to spend millions and millions of dollars on this. The only reason he'd agreed to the museum in the end was because Seth had promised that he'd take care of everything and Billy could just keep right on building bikes.

Kate nodded and took a few notes. "This will be a process," she warned him. "We could have a house under contract in a matter of weeks. The commercial property is much more involved—months of looking at properties, negotiating with sellers and dealing with architects."

Months of riding around with Kate, spending time with her when neither of them were under extreme duress. Months of getting to know her. Months of seeing that particular smile.

"Are you trying to talk me out of this?" God knew Billy had. He hated anything that distracted from building bikes.

And yeah, it was true that they didn't have a company without the bikes. But no one could compete in today's market without having a plan for the future.

So this was Seth's plan. He'd buy a house so he could be on hand to manage the museum project and the Bolton brothers. He'd prove that he had what it took to help the company and the family prosper.

That he had what it took to be a Bolton.

Kate's cheeks flushed as she dropped her gaze to the desktop. "No," she said quickly. "I just want you to go into this with realistic expectations." She looked up at him through her lashes. "It means we'll have to work together. A lot," she emphasized, as if the idea of spending more time with her was a deal breaker instead of one of the main reasons he was here in the first place.

Seth fought the urge to reach across her desk and cup her cheek in his hand. "Kate," he said in all seriousness, "why do you think I looked you up?"

Six

Kate was always polished and professional when she showed houses. Nobody wanted a real estate agent who was slovenly. That was just a fact. She was careful with her hair and makeup and put forth her best appearance.

But for this afternoon with Seth? She had gone above and beyond her normal preparations. She hadn't just carefully applied mascara—she'd primed and preened, showered and shaved until she was as glamorous as she could possibly be on her budget. If she'd had the cash, she would have gotten her hair blown out. As it was, she'd used hot rollers to tease her hair into a delicate half twist that she'd seen on Pinterest. It'd taken her a good half hour, which was a solid twenty-five minutes longer than she normally spent on her hair.

She was also thankful her best pair of trousers had buttoned. True, that button was straining as she drove her car toward the first house on the schedule for the day. If she were alone in the car, she'd undo the button and let her stomach relax.

But she wasn't alone. Seth Bolton was in her passenger seat, filling the space with his raw masculinity and leather jacket, tapping his fingers on his jeans. They were a dark-wash denim today, not nearly as scuffed as the black ones he'd worn the last time she'd seen him. And instead of a distressed T-shirt, he had on a gray flannel shirt. She'd never thought of gray flannel as a particularly attractive fabric before, but on him?

Yup. Keeping her button fastened and her baby bump sucked in.

Every day it seemed her clothing shrank just that much more. And for a woman who'd maintained a steady weight since she'd lost the freshman fifteen during her sophomore year, to suddenly be faced with a wardrobe that might not fit today and most definitely wouldn't fit tomorrow was more than a little daunting. Not to mention that she had to buy replacement clothes on a supertight budget.

She could tell by the way Seth fidgeted that he wasn't used to being a passenger but despite that, he hadn't changed the radio station or adjusted the mirrors or any of the other things Roger had always done every time she'd had to drive him home after he'd had too much to drink.

After all, Seth had arrived at Zanger Realty this morning on a motorcycle that didn't look familiar. Not that she remembered much about her wedding day fiasco, but she was certain that the bike hadn't been candy-apple red.

She'd never been into bikers before, but looking at that beautiful machine this morning as Seth straddled it, his hair tousled from the wind, those dimples in full force…

She shivered and pushed those thoughts aside.

She really needed Seth to buy a house. Even if his big ideas about the museum of motorcycles fell through, as long as he bought a nice house with a big piece of land attached, it'd be enough. But if there was something more…

She was being absolutely ridiculous as she turned onto the street of the first house. "We've got thirteen houses today," she warned him.

"Is that a lot? It seems like a lot," he said in a thoughtful voice before he turned that winning smile on her.

It was a good thing she was sitting because that smile was dangerous to her balance. "I've done more in a day. I don't anticipate you'll love them all."

"You mean, we might have to do this again sometime?"

Was she imagining things or did he sound happy about that prospect? "If you don't find something you like, we might."

"That would be too bad, wouldn't it?"

He was just a Good Samaritan, she reminded herself. A hot, kind, wealthy Good Samaritan.

He'd probably been a Boy Scout or something and this house-hunting expedition was the adult equivalent of helping an old lady across the street.

He'd comforted her on the day of her not-wedding. He'd made sure that she was safe and secure in a hotel that night. He hadn't taken advantage of her confusion or vulnerability.

Seth Bolton was a hell of a good guy. Maybe the best she'd ever known.

"Saturdays are usually free for me—after about eleven," he added. "We could have a standing date."

Oh, Lord—how was she supposed to react to that? "We might have to do that," she said, keeping her voice carefully professional. "Even if you love a house today, there are still the commercial properties to deal with."

A standing date didn't mean anything. Hell, it wasn't even a date. For all she knew, he always looked at women with that intensity. He probably wasn't flirting on purpose and besides—why would he flirt with *her*? She was pregnant and had not demonstrated the best of judgment. He might not hold abandoning Roger against her, but he'd be well within his rights to blame her for settling on Roger in the first place. Frankly, who could blame him?

So there wasn't anything here. He was using her as his real estate agent out of the kindness of his heart. It was a generous thing to do, but that was it.

She absolutely should not be thinking about Seth and dating in the same breath. No dating. He was a client. That was final.

How many times would she have to repeat that before she believed it?

"This property," she said as she pulled up in front of the split-level ranch in the Rapid Valley neighborhood because she was a professional and would not ask if his Saturdays were free because he was single, by God, "has a three-car garage." It was the only redeeming feature of the property, but she wasn't going to say that out loud. It was an ugly house. The shrubs were overgrown, the paint was peeling—absolutely no curb appeal, and she could tell from the pictures that the inside was in no better shape.

If it were up to her, it would be a complete teardown. But it wasn't. All she could do was sell the positives of any home. She almost hadn't put this house on the list, but sometimes seeing a house a client definitely didn't want helped clarify what they did, and since Seth had been vague about what he wanted—beyond no neighbors—she had to work from the process of elimination.

"So there would be plenty of room for a workshop and multiple motorcycles. Or a car, assuming you have one?"

"I own a car." He chuckled. "And a truck. Don't forget that I grew up in Rapid City. We have this thing called winter—maybe you've heard of it?"

She shot him a look. "I'm familiar with the concept."

Oh, there were those dimples again. She really needed to stop making him smile. "I also have three personal motorcycles, but I've been known to test out prototypes. It'd be great to have space for all of them."

In the week and a half since Seth Bolton had walked into Zanger Realty, Kate's dreams had gotten a lot more vivid. It wasn't like she hadn't dreamed of him before—she had.

Maybe it was the pregnancy hormones—that was her answer to every strange new change in her mind and body. Because her dreams now weren't just nonsensical images all jumbled together. Her dreams of Seth stripping her down—again—and this time instead of shaking her hand and riding off into the night, he laid her out on a bed and spent the evening feasting on her body.

She always woke up unsatisfied, with an edge of longing that no dream could fully erase.

Seth looked at the property. "It's kind of ugly."

"But there's a lot of potential," she pointed out. He slanted a side-eye look at her and she realized that she had said that with a little too much fake enthusiasm. "Okay, it's a little ugly. But there are things you can do to make it less hideous."

"You're really selling it," he said drily. "I guess we should look inside?"

"Never judge a book by its cover," she agreed.

He snorted. "The Boltons are a family of bikers. They look like mercenary criminals but underneath, they're all great big teddy bears." He paused, hand on the handle. "Don't tell my dad I called him a teddy bear."

She laughed as they got out of the car. "It's all confidential," she reminded him.

The split-level ranch did not improve in appearance outside the car. "It better have one hell of a kitchen," Seth commented, kicking at the unmowed grass.

Kate winced. Well, now she knew that a good kitchen was important. "Don't see what it is. See what it can be."

Seth scowled at her. "The other twelve aren't this ugly, are they?"

"No. I don't normally tell people this, but we're going in order from what I think you're least likely to buy. But," she added before he could suggest skipping half the list, "I've been wrong before. People can be surprising in what they want, and I don't know you well enough yet to be able to say definitively what you'll like and what you won't."

Seth's gaze snapped to hers and there it was again, that tension between them that hummed like a string, and Kate's brain took that moment to remind her this was the man who'd stripped her skirts off her and gotten a full view of her wedding thong.

He took a step closer. "I imagine," he said, his voice low, "that if we make this a standing date, you'll figure out what I'm looking for real quick."

She could feel the heat in her cheeks, but she couldn't look away, couldn't put any distance between them. "I imagine I will," she murmured.

His eyes darkened, and he looked dangerous in the very best sort of way.

Against her will, her body pitched toward his. His lips parted—he had nice lips, full and warm and...

"Kate." His voice stroked over her name like a lover's kiss as he took another step closer.

"Seth," she replied. It came out high and breathy.

Good God, what the hell was she doing? She couldn't—really, she *couldn't*. She was pregnant and coming off a failed long-term relationship and he was a client and…and…well, there were just a lot of really good reasons why she couldn't act on any of her fantasies right now.

She pulled away before she did something idiotic, like throw herself at him. "We…" She cleared her throat and tried again in her real estate agent voice. "We should go inside."

Some of the heat in his gaze cooled. "We should," he agreed. But he didn't sound happy about it.

And he didn't get any happier as they toured the house. The place was just as hideous on the inside as it was on the outside. The kitchen still had original appliances, the carpet was probably early 1980s—a cream color that had dimmed to a dull gray with grime. The wallpaper was peeling in the bathroom, and the tub was the stuff of horrors.

Kate cleared her throat. "As you can see, there is room to grow."

Seth snorted again. "But what? Is that mold, do you think? You shouldn't be breathing this air." He ushered her out of the bathroom, his hand on the small of her back. When they were in the hallway, he didn't remove it.

"You have to look into the future. Do you want room for a girlfriend or a wife?" She swallowed. "A family?"

His hand dropped away from her waist. "I don't have any plans for family anytime soon and I'm not seeing anyone," he told her. He stopped in the middle of peeking into the linen closet. "How are things going? With the pregnancy, I mean."

Kate blushed from the tips of her ears to her toes. "Good." Aside from her parents and Roger and Harold, few people knew she was pregnant. It had been hard enough to explain to everyone why the wedding was off without the added complication of an unplanned pregnancy. She had wanted to keep it quiet for long as long as possible.

Which meant she wasn't very good at talking about it yet.

Seth peeked into the third bedroom and winced in horror at the walls. "Is Roger going to step up?"

"In his way," she admitted. "He's been willing to provide child support."

Seth heard what she didn't say. "But nothing else?"

The concern in his eyes did things to her that had nothing to do with his dimples or her inability to stop blushing. He cared, damn his hide. He cared about her and her pregnancy, and she had the urge to tell him about all the strange things happening to her because he was the only person who'd asked. "No. We should look at the basement."

They went downstairs. The heart-of-pine paneling had seen better days, just like everything else in this house. "So he's not going to be a father to his child. Typical."

Kate was surprised by the bitterness in Seth's voice. "That's an accurate assessment of the situation," she said. When he gave her a hard look, she added, "Which is for the best, honestly."

"If you say so." He surveyed the rest of the basement room, his hands on his hips. "I think we're done here. We can cross this off the list."

"Done." They headed outside. "No more split-level ranches?"

"Good Lord, no," he said, getting back into the car. "I like the idea of having room to grow, though. There's always the possibility of house-guests, at the very least. Julie might come over."

She nodded and tried not to imagine what sort of houseguest this Julie would be. Young, pretty and not pregnant, most likely. Kate shook her head trying to get images out of her mind and focused on her job—the job she desperately needed.

She wished she could show him her favorite house—the one in the Colonial Pines neighbor-hood that had been on the market for almost a year. If she'd been able to afford it, she would have snapped that home up in a heartbeat. But even with combining her and Roger's incomes, the house on Bitter Root was out of reach—it was over twice the price of homes like this one and she didn't want to push Seth into more house than he wanted.

So she put that house out of her mind and focused on her job. "We have other options. One down, twelve more to go."

Seth groaned.

Seven

"I take it from the expression on your face that this one's a no, too?"

Seth was all for wood-burning stoves, but not ones that left scorch marks up a wall and dark shadows on the ceiling. "How is it possible that the house hasn't burned down?" Even as he said, his foot hit a particularly creaky board and he hoped like hell he wasn't about to fall through.

Kate sighed and put a hand to her lower back. "These are the houses at this price range," she began, closing her eyes and stretching.

"Then we go up." He had the money.

Even though Seth and his mom had lived comfortably—more than comfortably—for ten years with Billy Bolton, old habits died mighty hard. Seth had been looking at the cheaper end of homes simply because there was a part of his brain convinced that was all he should spend on a house.

That part of his brain was wrong. He could afford homes that cost four times the ones they'd spent the day staring at.

He was a partner in a wildly successful business. He had to start thinking like one. And living like one, too. Which would be good for Kate, too. A more expensive house for him would be a bigger commission for her.

He watched Kate sway as she massaged her lower back. They had walked through thirteen houses—only three of which were even remotely habitable. And she was pregnant. He had kept her on her feet all afternoon and clearly, she was tiring.

God, he was a cad. He wished he could make this easier on her. But he wasn't going to buy a mediocre house just so she wasn't on her feet as much.

Not that she looked pregnant. Instead, she looked *lush* and it took most of his willpower to keep from touching her. Her hair shone and her figure—she was a perfect hourglass. A voluptuous, decadent hourglass figure that he wanted to appreciate properly.

But he didn't. He was a gentleman, by God. But then she made a moaning noise and what was left of his willpower went up in smoke.

He stepped in close and pushed her hands aside. This was a bad idea, and yet he settled his hands on her hips, rubbing his thumbs in circles along the small of her back, and damned if she didn't feel right under his touch.

"Would you buy any of these houses?" he asked, trying to focus on relieving her tension instead of the way her body filled his hands.

For a long second, she didn't respond. She held her back straight, and her arms awkwardly hung at her sides. But then he must've found the right spot because all of a sudden, she sighed heavily and leaned back into his touch. "I would not," she admitted. "But my housing needs are different than yours. If I were to buy a home, it'd need to be a family home."

"Where are you living now? Not with Roger, right?" When Seth had found her at the scenic overlook, she had made it very clear that she couldn't go back to the place she'd shared with Roger. Seth knew that she had been at the hotel for a week—because the room had been charged to his credit card. But where she'd gone after she'd checked out, he didn't know.

"No, not with Roger." She sighed again, leaning back into him some more. "We... You shouldn't..."

"Hush," he said, closer to her ear than he should've been. She was right—he shouldn't be touching her like this and certainly not in a crappy house he wasn't going to buy. Funny how that wasn't stopping him. "Was this the last house?"

She nodded, not pulling away as he worked at her tired muscles.

"I'm taking you to dinner. No argument," he said quickly when she jolted. "We'll discuss real estate things. But I'm hungry and you need to get off your feet."

He could feel the tension in her body and there was a moment when he knew she was going to say no. And really, why had he asked? He was tired, too. He'd been sociable and chatty all afternoon and he should've been absolutely done with other people.

Instead, he was kneading her tired muscles and hoping she'd say yes. To dinner, that was. Nothing else.

But she wasn't going to. He let go of her hips as she stepped away from him. When she turned, her eyes were in shadows. "Dinner?"

It wasn't a no. He wanted to take her to an expensive place, with haute cuisine and complicated wine lists. He wanted to show her he was more than a biker, more mature than any other twenty-five-year-old. God knew he had the money now to wine and dine her. Hell, he could buy a restaurant for her if she wanted.

Suddenly, he realized he didn't want to take her to a fancy place. Yeah, he wanted to impress her—but for some reason, it also felt important that he show her who he really was.

And who he really was, was a biker. A multimillionaire business owner, yeah—but choppers were his life. "Sure. There's a great burger place not too far from here, but it's whatever you want."

She tucked her lower lip under her teeth and worried at it. The effort it took not to stare was surprising. "I should buy you dinner," she announced. "You paid for the hotel."

No way was that happening. "The hotel was a wedding gift. A not-wedding gift," he corrected with a smile when she opened her mouth to argue. "Dinner's on me. What are you in the mood for?"

He hadn't heard a no yet—but he still hadn't gotten a yes, either. "I'm sure you have someone you'd rather have dinner with."

Well, wasn't *that* an interesting statement? Was it possible that Kate Burroughs was jealous? It was, of course. But—jealous of who?

Then she answered the question for him. "This Julie—she's probably waiting on you?"

Seth knew it was not a good idea to laugh at an expectant mother. He fought it as hard as he could, but he lost ground little by little. His lips twitched up and then they broke open into a wild grin and the next thing he knew, he was chuckling.

Kate looked indignant. "What's so funny?" she demanded, crossing her arms in front of her chest.

The sight of that had Seth standing straighter at attention. "Julie's my little sister. She just turned ten. She's a year younger than Clara, and almost the same age as Eliza. We're all cousins." At this point, he couldn't explain his family tree without a whiteboard and color-coded markers. The all-purpose designation of "cousins" would have to do. "They are a tough pack of middle-school girls. You should see them play soccer sometime—they're brutal."

He didn't know what she had expected him to say, but it was pretty clear that wasn't it. Kate's mouth opened and then shut, her brow furrowed, then her mouth opened and shut again.

Seth smirked and took her by the elbow, leading her out of the house that might well burn down tomorrow. Gallantly, he opened the driver's-side door and bowed her into her seat. "You have two minutes to decide if you want burgers or not. I'm hungry."

It took less than two seconds before Kate said, "I would kill for some french fries," in a tone of voice that made it sound like french fry cravings were a crime. "Does this place have ice cream?" she asked hopefully.

"Malts *and* milkshakes."

She sighed, a noise that shot straight through him. "Burgers it is."

In short order, they were sitting in Seth's favorite booth at Mike's All Night Diner. Kate looked around nervously because Mike's was not quite a bar, but it was popular with a certain clientele. In fact, her car had been the only car in a parking lot full of bikes. But this was a family restaurant. People came here to eat. If they wanted to get drunk and brawl, there were bars for that.

"You come here often?" she asked as a guy in motorcycle leathers walked past them.

Seth shrugged. "Often enough. Don't forget, I own part of a motorcycle company. This was normal when I was growing up."

In fact, now that he had her here, he wasn't sure that this was a good idea. The odds of him being recognized by one of his dad's buddies were pretty decent and this could be an intimidating crowd. Kate stuck out worse than a thumb, sore or not, and word would probably get back to his dad.

Damn.

She really didn't belong in a place like this. He should've taken her to a classy place, with linen tablecloths and snooty waiters and artistically displayed food on oddly shaped plates.

Then again, he'd been so busy since he'd officially returned to Rapid City that he hadn't had time to catch up with the old gang. It just wasn't a priority—not right now, anyway.

Not that he would ever admit it out loud and certainly not in a joint like this, but Seth had missed his sister and even his parents. However, the phrase "you can't go home again" turned out not just to be a tired cliché but an absolute truth. Seth loved his family, but he didn't fit in their household anymore.

Still, he hadn't seen a single home today that made him want to give up his suite of rooms at the Mason Hotel. There, at least, he could come and go as he pleased, the bed was always freshly made and if he ate out too much, well, it wasn't that different from how he'd lived in LA.

The waitress took their orders—Kate went with a chocolate shake and Seth ordered an extra side of fries. Once they were alone again, he waited.

She didn't make him wait long. "Can I ask you a question?"

God only knew where this would go. "Of course."

"How old are you?"

Seth notched an eyebrow at her. "Does it matter?"

He had the feeling she was older than he was—not much older, but she might be anywhere from twenty-five to her early thirties. And really, was that such a big leap from twenty-five? No. It wasn't. It wasn't like he was thinking improper thoughts about a grandmother, for crying out loud.

He cleared his throat and shifted in his seat. It wasn't like he was thinking improper thoughts about her at all. She was his real estate agent. The only thing that mattered between them was that she helped him find the right properties.

Yeah, right.

"No, no," she defended weakly. "It's just that you seem a little...old to have a sister who's only ten."

He couldn't stop the smirk if he wanted to. "Technically, she's my half sister. My mom married into the Bolton family when I was fourteen."

He could see her doing the math in her head. It really wasn't complicated—except, of course it was. And he still didn't have a whiteboard to help explain the ways the Bolton half of his family overlapped with the Lakota half.

"Oh. I just assumed…"

"That I'm really a Bolton? I am—Dad adopted me. But I'm also a full-blooded member of the Pine Ridge Lakota tribe." He hoped that was enough of an answer for her, because he didn't want to get into his birth father, the sperm donor. Not at Mike's, not ever.

She dropped her gaze to the table, and he saw that she was nervously twisting the straw wrapper around her fingers. Seth had a moment of panic—his heritage wasn't going to be an issue, was it? He'd grown up on the reservation with his tribe, where he'd been loved and protected and then, when Billy had adopted him, the Bolton name—and reputation of his dad—had shielded him from the worst of the bullying off the reservation.

But that didn't mean he didn't know racism existed, in both subtle and overt ways. Once he'd left the rez, he'd seen how kids at his new high school had talked about other Native kids. He heard stories from his friends on the rez. And his dad had made damn sure he knew how to defend himself.

Part of that defense mechanism was not announcing his heritage until he was sure of his reception. And sometimes, that meant he never found the right time to tell a paramour before the relationship drifted away.

Within his family, his ethnicity wasn't just accepted, it was normal. *Welcomed.* His dad and his uncles came to powwows and helped out at the school on the rez and had married into the tribe. They hired Seth's uncles and cousins and friends from the rez to work in the factory. It all overlapped and blended together. Just like it had in Seth.

They'd never demanded that to be a Bolton, he had to give up being a Wawausuck. His legal name was Seth James Wawausuck Bolton. He was safe to be both, and that freedom was not something he took lightly.

It shouldn't matter what Kate believed, really it

shouldn't. Because there was nothing more than a professional business relationship between them.

Except…

Except for the way she'd leaned into his touch as he'd rubbed circles on the small of her back. And the way she'd looked when he'd stripped the petticoat off her. And the way her entire face had lit up when he'd walked into her office—and that was before he'd told her why he was there.

Okay, it mattered, what she thought. It mattered a lot.

Kate opened her mouth just as the waitress arrived with their food and said, "Anything else?" as she unloaded enough french fries to feed an army.

Seth eyed the plates of food. Mike didn't mess around with his burgers, and the malt was huge. There was easily enough food for five on the table, but Kate was staring at it with something that looked like devotion. "I think we're good," he said.

The waitress left and Seth turned his attention

back to Kate. She was staring at him openly. "Is it a problem?" He wasn't talking about the food.

"Of course not," she said easily. But she looked worried. "It's just…"

She picked up a fry and slid it slowly between her lips as she nibbled at the tip.

Who knew that eating french fries could be so erotic?

"You obviously have a really complex family history," she finally said.

Seth snorted. "That doesn't begin to cover it." Which was not an observation that let him relax. Crap, why had he brought it up at all? Oh, right—because Kate had thought Julie was a girlfriend and it had been important to make sure Kate knew that wasn't true.

He sighed and picked up his burger. Deep thoughts about identity and fathers could wait. "Eat, Kate. I know you're starving." And one fry at a time wasn't going to make much of a dent in this meal.

They made good headway into the food. Kate ate delicately—but she ate, thank God. Finally, she said, "I'm glad you came for me at Zanger, Seth."

"Are you?" Because there were several different ways he could interpret that statement. She might be happy about the commission, the chance to say thank you for the hotel room or…

"I'd been wondering about you," she replied, not quite meeting his gaze.

He let that statement settle around the table as he scooted the extra fries toward her. She'd cleared her plate. "In a good way?"

She nodded. "I…" She took an especially deep breath. "Most people wouldn't have done what you did for me."

Which part? Depositing her safely at a hotel? Or stripping off her petticoat? "I think you underestimate people."

That got a rueful chuckle out of her. "No, I don't. I almost married Roger. And you haven't even met my father. People like you are rare, Seth." She looked at him through thick eyelashes. "You're special. You just don't realize it."

That sure as hell seemed to answer at least one

question. A question that set his blood to pounding in his veins.

His hands itched to settle around her waist again. She wanted special? Hell, he could show her special. Slow and tender and hot and very, very *special*.

He put the brakes on those thoughts—something he was doing a lot around her. She was not technically available. She was expecting and they were working together and he didn't have any interest in being a rebound.

Well, not a lot of interest, anyway. But when she looked at him like that he had to admit that yeah, maybe he was a little interested.

"You know what I think?" he said, snagging a few more fries.

"Split-level ranches are the work of the devil?"

He snorted and damn near choked on a fry. "That, too. But seriously—I think you don't realize how special *you* are."

Her cheeks shot past a delicate blush and straight on over into red. "I'm not special. I'm a mess. You know that."

He considered that statement. "The situation is messy, maybe. But," he went on as she gave him an arch look, "that doesn't make you a mess. You believe leaving Roger at the altar makes you an utter failure, and when I look at you, all I see is one of the strongest, bravest women I've ever met."

She gasped, a hand covering her chest, right over her heart. "Seth…"

"No, I'm serious." He wasn't going to let her undermine her worth. "You walked away from a crap marriage and gave up your family business, right?"

She nodded, her eyes getting suspiciously bright.

"You know why? Because you're going to have a baby and you'd do anything—*anything*—to give that child the very best life possible. To walk away from everything you know, even though you know it's going to be hard—because it's the right thing to do? You amaze me, Kate. You simply amaze me."

Aw, hell. Sincere compliments were a bad idea,

because now she was crying. Quiet tears slipped down her cheeks, and he couldn't stand that.

He leaned over the table and cupped her face in his hand, swiping at her tears.

"I'm sorry," he said softly. "I didn't mean to make you cry."

"Don't you dare take that back." She sniffed, grabbing a napkin and dabbing at her eyes. "That's the nicest thing anyone's ever said to me."

Wasn't that a shame? Her former fiancé, her father—had anyone ever noticed who Kate really was?

He sat back as she took a bunch of deep breaths and got herself under control. "Sorry—hormones," she said, giving him a watery smile.

"Don't apologize. It was rude of me to ambush you with compliments."

That got him a slightly less watery smile. "It was, wasn't it?"

A strange silence settled over the table and then a movement behind Kate caught Seth's eye. Oh, hell—it was Jack Roy, one of Billy Bolton's oldest friends. Seth gave a friendly nod of his head to Jack, hoping the man would just keep moving without stopping.

No such luck. "Seth! Finally out and about?" Jack stood over the table, grinning down at Kate. "And who do we have here? Hello, beautiful."

Later? Seth was going to stab the man. Repeatedly. Jack Roy was a born flirt and had the kind of face a lot of women went for. And now he was smiling down at Kate and she was blinking up at the man, stunned by the force of his smile.

"Jack," Seth said, hearing the tension in his voice but seemingly unable to sound any more relaxed, "this is Kate Burroughs, my real estate agent. Kate," he went on, mentally willing Jack to get the hint and leave, "this is Jack Roy, head painter at Crazy Horse."

"And a whole lot more," Jack murmured in a seductive voice that Seth had heard him use on every female he'd ever met.

Kate's cheeks colored again as she dropped her gaze to the table. Crap, this was terrible. Not only was Jack interrupting just as things had gotten interesting, now the man would probably call Dad up and ask if Billy knew Seth had been having dinner with a pretty real estate agent. How much had Jack caught? Had he seen Seth cup Kate's cheek? Or wipe away Kate's tears?

Damn it all. Seth pivoted and launched a careful kick in the direction of Jack's shins. The man flinched but, to his credit, didn't even let out a stream of obscenities.

Instead, he turned that smile up to full power. "You make sure this one treats you right," he said, a hint of steel behind his seductive voice as he nodded at Seth.

Kate's eyes widened in surprise. "Oh, no—we're just working together."

The quick defense pricked at Seth's pride, even if it was exactly what she should have said because it was the truth. "I'm buying a house," he added.

By God, if Jack made some sort of crack about how Seth was all grown up and a big boy now, the man's handsome nose would never look the same.

Jack's mouth opened and then he closed it.

"Well, then," he said, notching a knowing eyebrow at Seth. Hopefully Kate couldn't see it. "I'll let you two get back to *business*." He reached down and appropriated one of Kate's hands, bowing over it. "Ms. Burroughs, it has been a true pleasure." Then the bastard kissed her knuckles.

A rumbling noise startled everyone at the table. It was only when both Kate and Jack turned to look at Seth that he realized the noise—a growl—was coming from him.

Jack's mouth curved into a knowing grin and Seth realized he'd walked right into Jack's trap. The jerk had intentionally provoked Seth with that kiss.

"Jack," Seth managed to get out without strangling the man.

"Seth—be good," Jack said with another wink before he finally, finally left.

Seth scowled at the man's back as he walked away. When he glanced back over at Kate, she was staring at him with what looked uncomfortably like confusion on her face.

Well, this evening was shot to hell. And he

wasn't even sure what he'd wanted before Jack had interrupted. This wasn't a date—Kate had said so herself. This was business.

This wasn't personal.

"Come on," Seth said, leaving a fifty on the table. "I think we're done here."

Eight

The ride back to the real estate office was tense. Or maybe that was just how Kate felt—because there was no missing the tension. Her dinner sat heavy in her stomach, and her head was a muddled mess. Her back hurt, her feet weren't any better and she was so tired she could barely see straight.

She just wanted to go home and go to bed and, inexplicably, she wanted to do so curled in Seth's arms. She wanted that *so* badly.

What kind of hormonal torture was this? There was no good reason why she should be craving

Seth's arms around her, his chest pressed against her back. As fantasies went, it was downright boring.

Except if she went to sleep in his arms, then she'd wake up there and then...

No, *no*. She was not following that train of thought to its logical conclusion. Not a bit.

It wasn't that she'd been scared when that friend of his had shown up. The guy was obviously a smooth talker who considered himself God's gift to women—not that he'd done anything for her. Because he hadn't. She'd been able to empirically realize he was an attractive man but compared to Seth, he was like a cardboard cutout next to a real man.

Then there'd been that kiss on her hand. If Kate didn't know any better, she would've thought that kiss had been to intentionally provoke Seth. There hadn't been a single bit of heat to Jack's lips—but when Seth had growled?

That noise had shot right through Kate, primal and raw. God, it'd sounded so *good*. Almost like he'd wanted her and was more than willing to fight for her.

But to what end? She and Seth were not together and no one present was a caveman. In her experience, no one fought over her. Hell, Roger hadn't even bothered to be upset when she'd jilted him.

This was only the third time they'd ever met face-to-face. The first time, she had been a hysterical runaway bride. The second time, she'd been too stunned to put together two coherent sentences. And today…

Today, he'd told her he wanted to buy a much more expensive house—which came with a much bigger commission. He'd rubbed her back and bought her dinner.

She was not the kind of girl to rebound with the first hot guy she saw. Or the second. Or any guy. Kate Burroughs did not do anything so impulsive or crazy or…fun.

Right. That was final. No fun. She was not interested in Seth.

It didn't matter that he just kept right on drifting through countless dreams, ones that always started with him riding up on his chopper before moving to him undressing her to hot, passionate lovemaking to…

Holding her while she slept. Making sure she felt safe.

Stupid hormones. She didn't want to do anything that would jeopardize their business relationship because she needed this business relationship more than she needed an attractive, wealthy man to rub her back.

They pulled up in front of the real estate office. Kate turned off the car but neither of them made a move to get out. Instead, they sat in silence and Kate had no idea if it was awkward or not.

"So," she finally began, unable to take the tension for another moment. "We looked at all the houses that were under two hundred and fifty thousand dollars. Do you want go up to three hundred thousand?" That was what most people did. They could handle increases of twenty-five to fifty thousand dollars at a time. And as much as she needed this commission, she didn't want to make this all about her.

But Seth wasn't most people. "I can't imagine there's a huge jump from what we saw today with a couple thousand dollars. Let's look in the three-fifty to five-hundred range."

She took a slow breath. The house on Bitter Root was four seventy-five. Would he like her favorite house or not? "Half a million is a lot of money, Seth. There's no need to buy more house than you'll use." Certainly not because of her. She didn't want to bankrupt the man just because he had a soft spot for…

Well, not for her. For pregnant women, maybe. But not for her.

He turned, facing her fully. There was something in his eyes—the same sort of almost possessive look he'd had when he growled earlier.

Heat flashed through her body as he stared at her. He'd looked earlier like he was willing to fight his friend over her. He looked very much the same now.

"We can't do this," she heard herself say before she completely lost her mind.

He lifted his eyebrows, and she immediately felt stupid. "Do what?" he asked, almost—but not quite—pulling off innocence.

"I'm not looking for a relationship." Well. So much for not making this awkward.

"Fair enough." He turned even more, resting one elbow on the dashboard and another against the back of the seat. "What are you looking for?"

Oh, hell. That was a question she most definitely hadn't seen coming. "I'm sorry?"

"You have to admit, Kate—there's something between us. I went to your office because I need to buy a house and an industrial property—but those weren't the only reasons." He leaned toward her—not close enough to touch her, but his gaze drifted over her and he inhaled deeply. "I couldn't stop thinking about you. I know that how we met wasn't exactly normal—"

Kate rolled her eyes. That was being generous.

"Look, I'm not in the market for a relationship, either," he went on, politely ignoring her unladylike response. "I don't plan on sticking around all the time. Settling down isn't in my blood."

Wasn't that what he'd basically said before? He was buying a house he only planned to live in for maybe six months out of the year? No, Seth Bolton wasn't the kind of guy who started playing house on a whim.

But still, hearing it baldly stated like that was physically painful, like someone was jabbing her hand with a pin. "What are you saying?"

"I need a house and you need a commission. That's all there has to be. But if you want something more..." His gaze darkened, and Kate swore it got ten degrees warmer in the car.

"More?" Her voice came out the barest of whispers.

She shouldn't be asking. She should, instead, get out of this car and thank him for his business and promise him that she would have a fresh slate of houses in a new price range that were sure to meet his needs by Saturday at 11:00 a.m. Their standing date.

"I think we want the same thing." His voice

was low and serious, and another flash of heat ran through her body. Ironically, she shivered. How was he doing this to her? She was not sexy—not after being on her feet all day and mowing through that many fries. She was not desirable—her pants barely buttoned.

Yet here Seth sat, looking at her as if she were the ice cream and he couldn't wait to start licking. Her body felt warm and liquid, like she could melt right into him. "You're not looking for long-term. You don't want to be hurt again and you've got a baby on the way to think about. But it might do you good…" His voice trailed off as his gaze caressed her face.

"*What* might do me good?" She was powerless to do anything but ask that question, because it appeared that all common sense had abandoned her in the face of one hot, protective biker dude.

He didn't answer her for the longest second and Kate thought she just might die on the spot. "Rebounds can be fun. Something short and sweet, no strings attached—something to help you get past those years lost to Roger. I think you deserve a little fun, Kate."

God, it sounded so good. So right. Because really—one conversation with Seth that didn't even involve touching, much less kissing, and she was already more turned on than she could remember being in years. Seth would be amazing. Simply amazing. Maybe the best she'd ever had, in her limited experience. And who knew what would happen after the baby came. She would be struggling to get through the long nights alone. Romance would be the last thing on her mind.

What if Seth were her last shot at romance—or even just good sex—for a long time? Years, even?

Was she willing to let go of that part of herself?

She wasn't, and she almost, almost said *yes* right then and there. Her mouth opened and the word was right on the tip of her tongue. *Yes*.

But she couldn't get it out because she wasn't the kind of person to willingly enter a sexual relationship just for the fun of it. Casual sex had never been casual. Not for her.

Still… "And you're fun?"

That smile—oh, she was not going to be strong enough. "I can take care of you, Kate. Even for a little while." His eyes darkened. "Just something to consider."

And the thing was, he seemed sincere about it. He wasn't boxing her in. He was focused on her, yes—but not intimidatingly so. "You're serious, are you?"

Please, let him be serious.

He nodded, the tip of his tongue touching his top lip. Jesus, she'd never seen anything so seductive. "You don't have to decide anything now. My offer's on the table. But promise me you'll think about it?"

She hated to ask this next question—but it was important she make a counteroffer. "And if I pass?" Because she needed the commissions he would bring in. She didn't want this to be some quid pro quo situation.

"Then you pass." He shrugged, as if rejecting his advances were no big deal. "Unlike some people, I know where the line is and I know not to cross it. I can keep business and pleasure separate."

Oh, that hurt. Because with Roger, they hadn't been separate. With Roger, she wasn't sure how much pleasure had been involved at all. The longer she was away from him—and her father—the more she was certain that Roger had only been with her because she came with the company.

Had there been any evidence to the contrary? No. There'd been no late-night calls, drunken or otherwise, professing that he really loved her and wanted her back. No daytime calls, either. No flowers. No big romantic gestures, like standing under her bedroom window and blasting their song until she realized she'd made a mistake.

Nothing. They didn't even have a song. When she'd asked what he wanted to play for their first dance, he'd shrugged.

And to think, she'd almost married *nothing*.

That did not mean that she wanted to jump into bed with Seth. It did mean, however, that the fact that he was making sense should be a source of concern.

So what if something short and sweet and fun sounded perfect? So what if it was Seth, who had made her feel safe from the very first moment she'd laid eyes on him? So what if the one man who seemingly gave a damn about her was the one offering to show her a good time—with no strings attached?

She had a baby on the way. There would always be strings attached.

"I can't," she said softly, unable to look at him when she said it. Because even if he was offering to make at least one of her fantasies come true, that wasn't her. Kate Burroughs wasn't that girl. She did what was expected of her and smiled and nodded and went along to get along. She did not have casual sex with a hot biker dude simply because it'd be fun and safe and so, *so* satisfying. That wasn't who she was.

Was it?

The silence in the car grew heavy and she didn't want to think about what would come next. Oh, she knew Seth wouldn't hurt her. Funny, how she trusted him with that. She simply didn't want the awkwardness. They'd laughed and joked and had an otherwise really lovely day together and she didn't want to ruin that.

"Then we won't. No harm, no foul." He didn't even sound upset by her refusal.

She peeked at him through her lashes. She didn't know what she'd been expecting, but that look bordering on concern wasn't it. Shouldn't he be mad? Insulted? Frustrated, at the very least?

Not concerned. Not for her. "And you're okay with it?"

He gave her a look as if she'd asked if he didn't like to kick puppies in his free time. "Why wouldn't I be? Besides…" he went on, leaning ever so slightly toward her. The tension between them tightened and she felt her own body move in his direction. "It's a woman's prerogative to change her mind."

And with that parting shot, he was gone before she could blink, out of the car and around to the driver's side and opening her door and—again— holding out a hand to her like he'd be honored if she joined him. "Otherwise," he said when she put her hand in his, his strong fingers closing around her own, "I'll see you at eleven next Saturday. We'll take more breaks and I'll buy you dinner again—no arguments, Kate," he scolded, cutting her off before she could protest. "I'm not going to run you into the ground."

And maybe it was the hormones or the exhaustion or the way he'd growled at his friend—or maybe it was the offer of something fun and easy—but whatever the reason, Kate didn't let go of his hand when she had her feet underneath her, nor did she step away from him.

She'd never known anyone like Seth Bolton, and she might not be able to make sense of what was going on in his head—because, again, he was attracted to *her*? But she was flattered and touched and interested all the same.

She shouldn't be, but she was.

Instead of putting distance between them, she held his hand and maybe even pulled on it a little, drawing him in closer. Not close enough to kiss, but close enough that she could feel the heat radiating off his chest, warming her on the chilly fall night.

"I'll…" She shouldn't say this but damn it, what the hell. "I'll think about it."

Seth's fingers tightened around hers and he favored her with a smile so dazzling she almost had to sit down again. "Do that," he said, his voice a caress on the wind. And just when she thought he was going to lean in and kiss her, he instead took a step back. "Until next week, Kate."

He waited until she'd gotten the office door unlocked before firing up his motorcycle and riding off into the dim light.

Oh, sweet merciful heavens—she really was going to think about this. About Seth and all those dream fantasies that had kept her company for the last several weeks. About how she might not get another chance for a lover for years because once the baby came, she'd devote herself to her child.

Would she really let this golden opportunity pass her by? And if she did, would she spend the rest of her life kicking herself for letting Seth Bolton slip through her fingers?

Was she out of her mind?

Nine

So that was a *no*, then.

Seth took one look at Kate and sighed. She was wearing a black pantsuit with a white blouse that was buttoned up almost to her chin. Her glorious hair had been scraped back into a severe ponytail and there wasn't a smile to be seen anywhere despite the fact that it was another lovely late-October Saturday. She looked more like she was on her way to a funeral than a house tour.

And if that didn't make her position clear enough, there was no missing the way Kate's pretty mouth twisted into a scowl when Seth walked into Zanger Realty at ten fifty-eight in the morning.

Definitely a *no*.

He shouldn't be disappointed. This had been the most likely outcome, after all. There was no getting around the reality of the situation, and that reality was that Kate was expecting and she didn't want to get involved with anyone.

He should be relieved. Her personal life was a mess and only an idiot would put himself in the middle of that. Her rejection was going to save him a lot of trouble and not a little heartache.

And yet—relief was not the feeling that had his stomach plummeting. No, he was not disappointed. And if he were, it was about the fact that he was going to be missing out on some great casual sex. After all, he didn't have to worry about getting her pregnant, right?

But that didn't explain the weight of sadness that settled around his shoulders. He and Kate could've been great together, but now? They'd never know.

Still, he was a gentleman and a man of his

word. He was not going to make this awkward, nor was he going to try to change her mind. He would not badger, nag or wheedle. He had no interest in being with a woman he had to wear down. He'd seen those kinds of guys in action in college and "pathetic desperation" didn't make anyone attractive. Good sex became great when everyone involved was equally enthusiastic about it.

So he straightened his shoulders and put on a friendly grin, even if it took effort to do so. "Good morning, Kate. What will we be looking at today?" Because the answer obviously wasn't each other.

Her scowl deepened as she stared at something on her desk. She looked positively insulted by his presence, which didn't make any sense. She hadn't even been insulted when he propositioned her. Shocked, maybe. Curious? Definitely. But not insulted. What the hell was going on?

"I have nine houses in your new price range on the schedule. We should get going."

The *no* couldn't have been louder if she'd

shouted it. What a shame. "Nine sounds good," he said, striving his hardest for friendly. "Thirteen was too much last weekend." She still wasn't meeting his gaze, so he charged ahead. "I made dinner reservations at the Main Course for six thirty, but if you don't think we'll be done before then, I can change the time." She hadn't been comfortable at the diner—or at least, she'd been okay until Jack showed up.

Tonight would be different. They'd have a quiet dinner, just the two of them and a bunch of house listings. No interfering family friends, no distractions.

Although, given the body language she was putting off, maybe they could use a few distractions. Because even closed down, she still called to him on a fundamental level that had nothing to do with reason or logic.

He'd made his offer last week because he'd convinced himself that he could show her a good time, no strings attached. But today? When the answer was no?

He should be able to let it go. He'd asked, she'd said no, end of discussion.

But looking at her now, he wasn't sure his offer had been only about her. Because he still wanted her. Desperately.

She hadn't answered yet. "Kate? We're still on for dinner, right?" He expected any number of polite excuses—she'd had a long night, she had other plans, she would be too tired. She had an actual funeral, thereby justifying the outfit. Something.

So when she looked at him through her lashes and said, "That sounds nice," in a tone that stroked over his ears like a lover's kiss, he didn't know what to make of it. And when she shot him a nervous smile before dropping her gaze again, he had even less of an idea.

Because that wasn't a *no*. It sure as hell wasn't a *yes*, either.

What if he was looking at a *maybe*?

Five hours later, he had absolutely no idea what to make of Kate Burroughs. Through eight other houses, she'd kept her distance, never getting within two feet of him. Not like he was going to grab her, but still. She was definitely not close enough to touch. No accidentally brushing hands as they stood in a narrow hallway—of which there were several. No putting his hand on her lower back to guide her out of a room. No gentlemanly offers of his hand or his arm for her to lean against as they walked over uneven paver stones.

However, every single time he'd glanced at her, he'd caught her watching him. She always looked away quickly, as if she were going to pretend she hadn't been staring, but he could feel her gaze upon him. She'd also thawed—slowly at first, but she'd gotten noticeably warmer to him as the day had progressed. She'd left her scowl behind at the first house—a markedly more habitable dwelling than nearly anything they'd looked at the previous week. By the third house, her lips had gone from a tight line to a gentle smile and by the fifth house, she was laughing at his jokes again. By the seventh house, her eyes softened and she let her gaze linger upon him when he'd glance at her, like she didn't want to look away.

She was still absolutely captivating.

He had to play this cool. As much as he desperately wanted to pull her into his arms and show her exactly how good they could be together, he didn't dare. She had to come to him, and besides—her decision was separate from their business dealings.

So he was doing his best not to think about anything other than real estate. It was a battle he wasn't necessarily winning, but he was trying.

"This isn't bad," he said, standing in the middle of a gleaming kitchen with a professional six-burner stove, a fridge with cabinet facings on the door and an island with a marble countertop. The whole thing was done in whites and grays with splashes of red and bright blue for accents. This was the last house of the day and they were on schedule, with a whole thirty-five minutes before their dinner reservations.

Kate snorted. "Four hundred and seventy-five thousand dollars and it's not *bad*?"

"Compared to what we looked at last week, it's amazing," he conceded.

He stood at the island, trying to get a sense for how the room flowed. And the fact that he was thinking about the flow of rooms was odd. He'd never considered work triangles and flow before. He and his mom had lived in a cramped two-room place before Billy Bolton had come into their lives, and then they'd moved into Billy's house and it'd been great simply because it was a real house with a room—and a bathroom—all his own.

The kid he'd been would take the first decent option he got. But he was a man of means now. He could afford to be picky.

He looked up at Kate, who was staring at the kitchen with open longing. Picky, indeed. "What do you think?"

"It's not going to be my house, Seth," she said in a quiet voice.

Something in her tone pulled at him. She sounded almost sad about that and he remembered what she'd said last week—she'd arranged for him to look at the least likely house first. This was the last house of the day, which meant she thought this was the best house they'd looked at yet.

"But you have a professional opinion, Kate. What do you think?" When she didn't answer right away, he added, "I'd appreciate it if you're honest."

About this kitchen, about the houses they looked at, about whether or not dinner was going to be painfully awkward.

About him. He wanted her to be honest about what she wanted from him. Just the commission or something else?

When she still didn't answer, Seth wished he could take it back. He never should've offered her a sexual relationship last week. He should've left it at flirting and making her smile, at making sure she was landing on her feet.

But then Jack had shown up and watching him hit on Kate had been more than Seth could take. She was *his*, not Jack's and not Roger's.

Except she wasn't. She wasn't a possession he

could do with what he pleased. She was a complicated woman who had her own life to live.

"I'm just asking, Kate. Your opinion is important to me. Just tell me what you think. I've never done this before."

"You've never bought a house before?"

"That, either."

Her lips twisted to the side in a scowl that he now recognized as confusion. "You've never propositioned a pregnant older woman before?"

Finally, they were at the heart of the matter. "Oddly enough, no. There's a first for everything, isn't there?" He gave her a warm smile, hoping that would help.

He wasn't sure it did. "But you've offered to have no-strings relationships with other women?"

He tried to process the line of thinking behind that question. How long had she been with Roger? Kate didn't strike Seth as the kind of woman who'd had a lot of casual relationships. "I went to college."

The scowl was back. But at least this time he'd earned it. He braced for her cutting rejoinder, but instead she squared her shoulders and said, "This is an amazing house," in what he thought of as her real estate agent voice. "The master suite has that Jacuzzi bathtub and the office on the first floor has an amazing view. It sits on two acres so you don't have any neighbors within immediate line of sight and although it only has a two-car garage, there's more than enough room to expand or even build a separate workshop. The property is fenced so if you're ever going to have a dog or children, there would be a huge backyard for them to play in."

"It is a great house on paper," he agreed. "But I can read. I want to know what you think of the house, Kate."

"It was originally on the market nine months ago for five ninety-nine," she went on, ignoring him. "But was overvalued and the market has been a little soft at this price range. The owners are probably desperate to sell, so we might be able to get them down to four-fifty."

He might never figure this woman out, but he was going to have a hell of a good time trying.

"Kate." She swung around to look at him. "Do *you* like it?"

She blinked at him in confusion and he had to wonder, had anyone ever asked her what she liked before?

Then she exhaled heavily, looking defeated. He didn't like that look on her. "Roger and I…" she started, her voice trailing off. Then she tried again. "We'd already purchased a house when this came on the market and besides, it was out of our price range. But I've been through it several times now and…"

Her hand stroked over the marble countertop affectionately as she walked to the sink, making his gut tighten. He wanted her to touch him like that, to hear that longing in her voice when she talked to him.

Great. Now he was jealous of a house. Bad enough he was jealous of Jack, but at least that was another guy. The house was just a house.

She leaned against the sink and stared out the window into that big fenced backyard and damned if she didn't look like she belonged here.

She loved this house and for some insane reason, he wanted to give it to her.

"The house just makes *sense*," she went on, a note of defeat in her voice that he didn't miss. "The way the rooms are arranged, the way everything works together—it's one of the best houses I've ever been in. Nothing to compromise on, nothing I'd want to change. I've always been able to see myself living here. It'd be a wonderful place to raise a family."

He understood what she was saying. She hadn't been able to afford it even when she'd had Roger's income to kick in and now? Even if the price could be negotiated down more, it'd still be beyond her. Instead, she was going to have to watch someone else buy her dream home.

Unless… "Question." She turned, her eyebrows raised. "We haven't started on the industrial properties for the museum. What happens if I buy a piece of property for, say, four million dollars? Will your commission be enough to buy this house?"

The color drained out of her face, which was

not the reaction he'd been hoping to get. "Seth," she said softly, sounding even sadder—which had not been his goal. "You can't just snap your fingers and solve all of my problems. I got myself into my own mess and I am going to get myself out of it, too." She swallowed, her eyes huge. "I don't need you to save me."

"That's not what this is." But even as he said it, he wasn't entirely sure that was the truth. He didn't think about it in terms of saving her. He thought about it in terms of *helping.* Of course, why he felt this compulsion to help her was another question he didn't want to investigate too deeply right now.

"Then tell me what this is about. The truth, Seth."

The truth? Hell. The truth was he was worried about her. He couldn't stop fantasizing about her. He was glad she hadn't married Roger. He knew how hard single mothers had it and he didn't want it to be that hard for her. It shouldn't be that hard for anyone, but especially not for her.

He didn't say any of that. Instead, he closed

the distance between them and cupped her face in his hands. "This," he said, lowering his lips to hers, "is the truth."

Then he kissed her.

Ten

Oh, God—Seth was kissing her. And somehow, it *was* the truth.

Because the truth was, she wanted him to kiss her and more than that, she wanted to kiss him back.

How had she thought that she could talk herself out of this need? God knew she'd tried. For a whole week, she'd diligently reasoned that it didn't make sense to fall into bed with Seth Bolton. It was a bad idea and the list of reasons why was long. Safer to keep their relationship strictly platonic.

In fact, she had gotten up this morning determined not to let things get to this point. But now that they were here—now that he was brushing his lips over hers, soft and gentle and asking for permission...

She sighed into his mouth and wrapped her arms around his waist. However many reasons there were not to do this, none of them trumped the simple fact that she *wanted* Seth. She wanted to hold on to this last chance to be Kate Burroughs before her identity was redefined by motherhood. She wanted her baby, but she didn't want to lose herself, either.

So she kissed him back. She opened her mouth for him and slid her tongue along the seam of his lips and thrilled at the groan of desire that rumbled out of his chest. She pressed her body to his and let the warmth of his solid muscles sink into her skin.

She stopped trying to fight this desire. She stopped trying to fight herself.

Seth was the one who broke the kiss. He pulled back and rested his forehead against hers, his chest rising and falling rapidly. "I shouldn't have kissed you," he said, his words coming out in a rush. "But I can't regret it."

This was it, her last chance to stop this madness before it consumed her.

Too damned bad she wanted to be consumed. "Yes, you should've."

He gave her a quizzical look. "Was I reading you wrong? I thought you weren't interested."

She had tried so hard not to be. "Seth, this is a bad idea." His face fell. "But that doesn't mean I'm not interested. I don't *want* to be interested in you. My life is complicated enough. But I can't help wanting you."

Dimly, she was aware that they were locked in an embrace inside a stranger's home. True, the home had been unoccupied for months. But ethically, she was pushing her luck. "We need to leave."

He nodded and stepped back, but he didn't let go of her. Instead, his arm slid down around her waist and he held her tight to his side. "Where do you want to go? Dinner or..."

She would need to eat—eventually. But she needed him more. "Or?"

He guided her toward the door. "What about your place?"

She hesitated. It was such a small apartment. She knew she shouldn't be embarrassed for him to see it—it was clean and neat. But after spending the day in some of the nicer homes in Rapid City, her apartment would look pathetic in comparison.

Besides, she didn't want Seth in her apartment because then she would have all these memories of him there. Every time she walked into her bedroom, she would remember him stretched out on her bed, the sheet around his hips and his chest bare. Every time she tried to fall asleep, his presence would keep her awake.

She needed to keep a little distance between the rest of her life and what was going to happen in the next few weeks. Because she couldn't imagine that this would last more than a few weeks.

Just long enough for her to taste true passion. Just enough memories to keep her going through what would be a few years of long days and sleepless nights. That's all she was doing with Seth—making memories.

"Your place?"

"I'm currently living in a hotel. But," he added, opening the door for her, "it has room service. If you're sure?"

Was she sure this was a good idea? No. She was pretty sure it wasn't.

But was she sure that Seth would take great care with her? That he would deliver on exactly what he had promised—something fun and satisfying, something to erase the lingering bad memories of Roger from her mind? Something *good*?

She leaned up on her tiptoes and brushed a kiss across his lips—a promise of more to come. "I'm sure. Are you?"

That smile—confident and cocky, sensual and heated—*that* was exactly what she was looking for. "You have no idea."

Twenty minutes later, Seth said, "We can order room service later," as he guided her into the room and kicked the door shut behind him.

Then she was sinking into his arms and wondering why, exactly, she'd fought against this so hard. It didn't mean anything. She was attracted to Seth and he was attracted to her, and she simply hadn't had enough fun in her life for so long that she almost couldn't remember what it felt like to enjoy herself.

Well, to hell with that. Because she was going to enjoy this time here, with this man. "Okay?" Seth asked again as his hands settled around her waist. They hadn't even gotten to the bed—he was still leaned against the door. But he wasn't going to let her go.

"Okay," she agreed, sliding her hands underneath his jacket and flattening her palms against his chest. It had been unseasonably warm today and he had on another Crazy Horse T-shirt. His body was hard and hot under her touch, and touch him she did.

He let her. He stayed still while she explored the planes of his chest. He didn't yank her clothing off, didn't try to skip the foreplay and get straight to the sex. He let her take her time and that felt important. She didn't know how long they had together, but she didn't want to rush it.

"You never did tell me how old you are," she murmured as she pushed the jacket from his shoulders. He let go of her waist long enough for the leather to hit the floor and then she was studying his arms. She hadn't seen them before—the muscles that strained at the sleeves of his shirt, a tattoo visible on his right biceps. "Good Lord, Seth. Look at you."

"Twenty-five. And I'd rather look at you. Except…without these clothes." He peeled her black suit jacket off her shoulders. "Black and white are all wrong on you. You need bright, vibrant color, Kate. You're gorgeous in color."

She felt her cheeks get warm. "It was the only thing that fit," she admitted—and that was only because the pants had elastic in the back. Otherwise, she would've been showing houses in yoga pants.

"Ah. And here I thought you were sending me a message—hands off."

She could feel that her whole face had turned

red and it only got worse as he reached for the buttons on her slacks. It wasn't like he hadn't undressed her before—he had. He had lifted her skirt and peeled off a petticoat and been within inches of her most personal areas. But it was different now. Her body was changing faster every single day. "I'm different. Since the last time we did this."

His mouth curved into a dangerous half grin. "We've done this before? I'm sure I would remember."

"You know what I mean," she said, whacking him on the side of the arm. "You have undressed me before. At least partially."

"Trust me, babe—I have not forgotten. I never will." He worked the zipper down and then slid his hands underneath the fabric, along her skin. "And this time, I'm not going to settle on 'partially.'"

She didn't have on a thong today, nor did she have on stockings and a garter. The best she could do was a pair of bikini-cut panties—white—with a little pink bow on the front and her new, very serviceable white bra. The underthings were innocent, almost—the most innocent thing about this particular situation, anyway.

She could feel the palm of his hand moving over the fabric of her panties and then lower, over her hips. The slacks gave way as he stroked down her skin. He followed the pants, falling to his knees before her as she revealed her skin and this time, she couldn't drop a skirt to hide.

This time, she didn't want to.

They felt like they were starting from the same spot—but it was different, too. She hadn't known anything about Seth the first time she'd balanced a hand on his shoulder so she could step free of extraneous fabric. She hadn't known if he was rich or poor, old or young. All she had known then was that she was safe with him.

She still was. "Tell me what you want," Seth said when she had stepped free of the slacks. He grabbed them and threw them out of the way, then began to slide her trouser socks off. "I want to give you what you need."

Her eyes fluttered shut and she tried to put words to what that was.

She wanted to be selfish. She didn't want to swallow down her disappointment in bed to protect anyone's feelings. She didn't want to accept mediocre sex because Roger was incapable of putting forth the effort to get better. She didn't want to settle because it kept the peace.

She needed to know what Kate Burroughs wanted. She needed to know that person was valuable and desirable and worth the risk.

She needed Seth to fight for her.

She needed to fight for herself.

"Anything," Seth said as her other sock and shoe were also tossed aside. He sat back on his heels and ran his hands up and down her bare legs, warming her skin. "Be honest, Kate."

"I don't want to regret this," she said, because that was the most honest thing she could think of. "I don't want to regret you."

"You won't. And I won't, either," he assured her. He leaned forward and pressed his lips against her thigh. "I had the most erotic dreams after the last time," he whispered against her skin as he kissed his way up her leg.

"I'm different now. Everything's changed." She felt huge and she knew she was only going to get bigger. Rationally, she knew it was because of the baby, but it was still hard to know that an ugly black suit was the only thing she could wear for her standing date with Seth Bolton.

She didn't feel ugly now, not as Seth moved to the other thigh and began to kiss and nip at her skin. She watched in fascination.

"You were gorgeous two months ago, but now?" Seth leaned back and began to undo the buttons on her shirt. He had amazingly long arms, powerful muscles. Everything about him was powerful and he was here with her. How did this make any sense?

"But now?" he said in such a sincere voice that even though it didn't make any sense, she had no choice but to believe him. He got the buttons undone, and she shrugged out of the shirt, letting it fall. "My God, Kate—*look* at you."

She was going to protest that there was nothing to look at—at least not anything good—but he sat forward and pressed a kiss right below her belly button. And then one below that. And then one even lower. What started out as a sweet, tender gesture rapidly became something else entirely.

"Seth," she said, her knees beginning to shake as his mouth moved over the thin cotton of her panties, coming ever closer to her sex.

"Tell me what you need, Kate," he said, bringing his hands up to cup her bottom—and bring her closer to his mouth. "Do you need this?"

He skimmed his teeth over her panties, pulling the fabric aside. She was so shaky that she had no choice but to bury her fingers in his thick black hair and hold on. He looked up at her and squeezed her bottom, a knowing smile tugging at the corner of his lips. "Come on, Kate—you have to tell me."

"Yes," she whispered. He was slow and methodical—and focused entirely on her. He wasn't keeping an eye on the clock or an ear on the game. He wasn't wishing he were anywhere else. She had his undivided attention and that, more than anything else, was what she needed right now.

That and his mouth on her. "More." It came out half an order and half a plea.

His grin sharpened. "Good girl. I want to hear what you like." Then he buried his face against her sex.

"Ohh..." That. Definitely *that*.

Somehow, he pivoted her so instead of her standing, she was leaning against a wall. He scooted her legs a little farther apart and pressed himself between them. He still gripped her bottom with one hand, but with the other, he reached around the front and pulled her innocent-looking white panties to the side. Not off—just to the side. "How about this? Do you need this?" he asked, pausing just long enough that she knew if she said no, he'd stop.

She didn't want him to stop. "I do," she said, her voice little more than an exhale.

He kissed the top of her thigh, teasing her. "Are you sure?"

For some reason, the question irritated her. She was tired of people not listening to her, tired of them assuming they knew best. She wanted Seth to make her feel gorgeous and sexy, she wanted the release of a good orgasm—but more than that, she wanted him to listen. She wanted to be heard.

She tugged on his hair—hard—pulling him back to where she needed him. "I said yes," she hissed, watching as his eyes fluttered shut and he inhaled her scent deeply. "And I meant it. I won't beg, Seth. You're going to give me what I want and that's final."

He moaned. He was on his knees in front of her, his face buried against her sex, and he *moaned*. It was a noise of pure want and it shot straight through her. And then he kissed her, right where she needed his mouth. His lips moved over that nub of skin and nerves and then it was her moaning as she held him to her. His tongue flicked out and traced a pattern on her skin, one that she would feel for the rest of her life.

He was marking her, and she was his to be marked.

As his mouth worked her body, the rest of the world fell away. She stopped worrying about her rounded tummy or her woeful closet. Commissions and tours and kitchens—they all fell away. Even the fantasy that had been Seth—him stripping her at the scenic overlook and instead of putting her on a motorcycle, doing this exact same thing—it fell away because that hadn't been real. It'd been a bedtime story she'd told herself, a lie to convince herself that she was still Kate Burroughs and that was good enough.

This? This was not a lie. She was Kate Burroughs and Seth wasn't some mysterious, handsome stranger, he was a man—a warm, solid, flesh-and-blood man—who wanted her. More than that, he was putting her first. Hell, she hadn't even gotten his shirt off. She wanted to see his body, to touch it and taste it.

She wanted him all for herself. Not for anyone else, not for a commission. She wanted Seth Bolton because he was a man she liked, a man who cared about what happened to her. A hand-some, confident man.

A man who was very good with his mouth. There was something naughty about this. They hadn't made it to a bed—no one was naked. But there was something freeing about it, too.

"God, Kate—you taste so good," he murmured against her sensitized flesh, his words vibrating right through her. "Better than I imagined."

Well, they were being honest. "I dreamed of you doing this, too," she told him. The hand that was still on her bottom slipped underneath her pant-ies so he could grip her harder. It wasn't enough. She heard herself say, "I need more, Seth."

The request shocked her. Had she ever said that before? If she had, she was pretty sure it hadn't gotten the desired result. When had she learned that, even in bed, she had to be quiet and go along to get along? Whose bright idea was that?

"Mmm, something more." He leaned back. The next thing Kate knew, her panties had been pulled down and Seth was back between her legs. This time, in addition to his mouth, his fingers began to work her. He stroked up and down and found that sensitive nub again, teasing it with his teeth as he slipped a finger inside her.

The relief was so intense that she could've cried. He thrust that finger into her in time with the movements of his tongue and his lips, and it was everything she'd ever wanted and never gotten.

Then, just when she was sure she couldn't take another moment, he added a second finger and she was lost.

Eleven

Kate's grip on his hair bordered on painful, but Seth wasn't about to do anything to stop the incoming wave of her orgasm. He could take a little pain for her.

She was so beautiful when she came. Her color was high and her eyes were glazed over with lust. And her body? Damn, her body. There was something so lush and gorgeous about her that even though he was inside her, he couldn't get enough. He had never been this hard for a woman, never this desperate.

"Seth—Seth!" she gasped as her body convulsed around him. He leaned in, putting just a little more pressure against the spot that drove her wild. The noise she made—he wanted to capture it in a kiss and hold it deep inside him, but he didn't dare let her go.

Her back arched off the wall and then the crisis passed and she slumped, her legs giving out. He managed to catch her before she toppled them both over. "I've got you, babe," he whispered against her breast as he studied her.

For a long few minutes, they stayed in this awkward pose, him on his knees, her half draped over him. She was breathing hard, and he wasn't much better off.

He needed to move. It was torture to sit on his heels in these boots, torture to keep these jeans buttoned. He needed to lay her out on the bed and show her *that* had just been a preview of what was to come.

But when he shifted to stand and sweep her into his arms, he realized there were tears running down her cheeks. "Kate?"

She blinked at him. "Seth…" she murmured, sounding almost as confused as she looked.

"Oh, God—I'm sorry," he said, scrambling to his feet and pulling her into his arms. He crushed her in a hug and then realized perhaps *crushing* was not the best option right now, so he shifted to make sure he was merely holding her firmly. "I'm sorry," he repeated.

"What? No—no, you don't understand." She sniffed and pulled away, scrubbing at her cheeks with the back of her hand. "That was amazing, Seth. I don't think…I'm sorry. I'm not upset. It's the hormones. I've never— This isn't— I…" She trailed off, looking, if possible, even more confused.

Oh, thank God. He hadn't hurt her, hadn't crossed the line—hadn't misread the situation. "So you're okay?"

She smiled—a watery smile, but a smile all the same. "Honestly, I'm not sure if I've ever been better. It was amazing. You," she said, poking him in the chest, "are amazing. And wearing far too many clothes."

"I can fix that." He grabbed the hem of his T-shirt, but she batted his hands away.

"I want to do it."

"Never let it be said that I don't give a woman what she wants." He let his hands fall to his sides as she began to tug at his T-shirt. She was in no hurry, her movements languid and relaxed. Her tears had dried and all that was left was that knowing smile, satisfied and ready for more. He'd put that smile on her face and by God, he'd leave another in its place.

She pulled his shirt over his head and let it fall to the side. "Good heavens, Seth—you're stunning."

She skimmed her hands over his chest, brushing his nipples and taking the measure of his waist. He fought to keep the groan from escaping. "I aim to please."

She paused at the button of his jeans and shot him a look. "What about you? What do you want?"

The word *everything* popped up in his head before he could think. But he didn't say that, not out loud. This was short-term, fun. No strings attached. He could have everything, for a limited time only.

For some reason, the thought made him sadder than he expected. He didn't expect it to upset him at all, frankly. He expected to get lucky and have a good time and call it a day. He didn't *want* anything more.

Kate began working at his button fly, drawing his attention back to her. She was simply the most beautiful woman he'd ever seen. He wanted to burn that ugly black suit and deliver Kate to his aunt Stella, the fashion designer. He wanted to wrap her in vibrant blues and golds and greens. He wanted to see Kate in all of her glory, instead of her beauty hidden.

He pulled the ponytail holder out of her hair and sank his fingers into her locks. "Beautiful," he said as he arranged her silky hair around her shoulders.

She shoved his pants down and he kicked out of his boots. That left him in nothing but his boxer briefs—which were barely keeping his erection contained.

Kate straightened, a shy smile on her face. He knew she was no innocent, but there was still something unsure about her. Which she only reinforced when she asked, "Now what?"

He didn't particularly want to think about Roger Caputo right now, but again he had to wonder what the hell had been wrong with that man. Kate was a gorgeous, passionate woman and Roger had just let her go. Was he that damned blind that he couldn't see what was right in front of him?

If Kate were his, Seth would do everything in his power not just to keep her, but to keep her safe and whole and so blissfully happy that she never had to worry about anything.

Too damned bad she wasn't his.

"Bed," he said, having trouble thinking straight. He was personally familiar with the concept of lust—but this? This was different. More intense. He was *desperate* for her, and he had never been desperate before. Hard up, maybe. But not like this.

She ducked her head and turned toward the king-size bed. But Seth reached out and turned her back toward him. "Wait for me, babe," he murmured, drawing her in close so that he could feel her breasts pressed against his bare chest. He fisted his hand in her hair. Tilting her face to his, he brought his mouth down upon hers.

He kissed her with everything he had. She made a squeak of surprise but then she melted into him. She tasted so good—he couldn't get enough of her. And when her arms came around his waist and she slid her hands down to cup his ass, he got even harder.

He wanted to take his time with her—he *was* taking his time with her—but the intensity of his desire was blinding. He began to walk her back toward the bed, never taking his mouth from hers.

She came alive against him. He could almost see the moment when she forgot to be self-conscious and nervous. He could definitely taste the sweetness of that moment. He captured her little noises and need with his lips. He let go of her hair long enough to unfasten her bra and cast it aside, and then he had to look.

"Sweet Jesus, Kate," he groaned, cupping her breasts in his hands. They were full and heavy, her nipples a deep russet red. "Perfect," he said, brushing his thumbs back and forth over her tips and watching them tighten.

She gasped her arousal. "They're not usually that—oh, Seth," she moaned as he lowered his head to one and replaced his thumb with his tongue. "They got bigger. More—oh! More sensitive." Her hands found his hair and, just like she had held him to her sex before, she held him to her breast now.

The words were slow to penetrate the fog of desire in Seth's mind, but penetrate they did. More sensitive—that meant he needed to be gentle. It meant that if he played his cards right, he might be able to drive her to orgasm just by playing with her nipples alone.

The back of her legs hit the bed and she sat abruptly. Seth came off her breast with an audible *pop*. She blinked up at him, apparently surprised as to how she'd landed where she was. "Seth," she whispered. She stroked her hands down his chest, and his stomach—then she hooked her fingers into the waistband of his briefs and pulled.

They had all night. That was what Seth kept telling himself when his cock sprang free. He held his hands at his side, giving her the space to explore without making any demands. Because they had all night and he had nowhere he had to be tomorrow morning and by God, he was going to make this memorable for her.

"Wow," she said, tracing the tip of her finger along the side of his erection, making him quiver. "I had no idea." Seth was powerless to keep the growl inside.

Maybe he wouldn't despise Roger. True, the man had apparently never done anything good for Kate, but on the other hand, it was going to be easy—and enjoyable—to blow Kate's preconceived notions of sex and intimacy out of the water.

She wrapped her hand around his shaft and

stroked once, twice—all while staring at him intently. "Is it okay if I do this?" she asked, stroking him again.

"God, yes." Why wouldn't it be?

"I just…" But she didn't finish the thought. Instead, she stroked him slowly, driving him past the point of thinking. And that was before she leaned forward and pressed her lips to his tip.

And suddenly it was too much. Before she could take him into her mouth, Seth grabbed her by the hair and pulled her away. "I can't— Kate," he said, not even able to get a coherent thought out. He leaned down and crushed his mouth over hers, desperate to be inside her. But at the very last second, his lone remaining functional brain cell kicked into gear—the condom. It wasn't like he could get her more pregnant—but safe sex was good sex. He forced himself to pull away from her and went to grab his jacket, fishing the condoms out.

When he turned back to the bed, Kate was leaning on her elbows, watching him intently. There was something so right about her, about them being here together. *Everything*, he thought, staring at her. She was everything.

He prowled across the hotel room, kneeling on the bed next to her. He was supposed to be saying things to her, he was pretty sure—sweet nothings about how gorgeous she was, how excited he was—how great he was going to be for her.

He had nothing. Not a damned thing. And when she reached out and gripped his erection again, the need to be buried inside her was overwhelming.

He rolled on the condom and fit himself between her legs. "Yeah?" he asked, dragging his erection against the folds of her flesh.

Her hips arched into him as her eyes fluttered. "Yes, please," she whispered, wrapping her arms around his neck and bringing him close so she could sear him with her lips.

"So polite." He was going to push her past that. He wanted her demanding and bossy, confident in her desires and in his ability to fulfill them.

He shifted and found her opening and then, as carefully as he could, he began to thrust. Her body was tight around his and the sensations—damn, the sensations. He'd always liked sex. Careful sex, of course. He wasn't going to get anyone pregnant and leave them high and dry. He was *not* that guy. But sex itself had always been fun.

This? Burying his body inside Kate's went far past fun, he realized as they fell into a rhythm. Being with Kate wasn't a fun Saturday night. It was suddenly as vital to him as breathing.

She rose to meet him as he plunged into her again and again and he completely surrendered to her. Her hands gripped his shoulders, his arms. "Oh, God—Seth," she cried, her body tightening around his.

"Yeah, babe—yeah," he ground out, straining to keep his orgasm in check long enough. He wouldn't dare leave her unsatisfied. It simply wasn't polite.

She thrashed her head against the pillow and dug her fingernails into his back as her body gripped his with such strength that he couldn't hold anything back. He gave himself over to her and held on as she came.

He collapsed on top of her, both of them breathing hard for a few moments as his head cleared. This time, when he leaned back to withdraw, he was ready for the tears—because they were there again. She looked at him and smiled and then laughed and said, "It's good crying, I promise."

He was willing to take her at her word that this was a hormonal thing. "You never cried before?" he asked, getting rid of the condom and draping himself around her.

"No," she said, sounding tired and sated and happy. "Or laughed. But then, I don't ever remember having orgasms like that, either."

Roger was an idiot. A clueless idiot. "I am ever at your command, my lady."

She laughed again. "I think you were right."

He propped himself up on his elbow and began to trace her collarbone with his lips. "About what?"

She cupped her palm around his cheek and

lifted his face so he had to look at her. Her eyes sparkled. "I think you're going to be very good for me."

His chest puffed up with pride and he nipped at the space where her shoulder met her neck. "It was only the beginning, Kate. I can be even better for you than that in just a few minutes." He lowered his mouth to her breast again, but just then her stomach rumbled. He bit back his smile and leaned away, putting his hand on her stomach. If he didn't know she was pregnant, he wouldn't be able to tell. Soon, maybe. "Maybe we should have dinner first? I picked this hotel for the room service."

He would do anything for that smile of hers. Everything. "I'd like that."

Seth called in their orders while she got cleaned up in the bathroom. When she came back out wearing her boring white shirt again, he growled.

"I am not going to be naked when room service shows up, thank you very much. Besides," she went on as he stared at her legs, "you can always take it off again later."

"Woman," he groaned, falling back on the bed as if she'd shot him. "Come wait with me."

They curled up under the covers and turned on a game, although they didn't watch it. Seth was too busy touching her skin, massaging her shoulders, stroking her hair, to pay any attention to sports. By the time dinner showed up, he was more than half hard for her all over again.

And the whole time, he kept thinking that it was a damn shame that he had no plans to stay in Rapid City on a permanent basis. Though even if he were staying, he wouldn't want to keep this thing between them going. Kate didn't need a long-term relationship that was nothing more than casual sex. She needed a man who could settle down and stay in one place, someone who could be a good dad and shoulder his half of the load—if not more. She needed someone who would be there every night and every morning and that, sadly, was not Seth. He simply didn't have it in him.

He'd always been restless. Although his mom

had never said so one way or the other, Seth attributed his wanderlust to his birth father. The man had disappeared before Seth had been born, never to be seen on the reservation again. Seth had no idea if his father was kind or hard, laughing or serious. All he had ever known about the man was that he left his girlfriend and his unborn child behind without a second look.

That was why Seth's new position at Crazy Horse Choppers fit him so well. He'd already spent a year in Los Angeles, hobnobbing with the rich, famous and the wished-they-were-famous. His uncle Bobby was always looking for the next big thing. Billy just wanted to build motorcycles. Ben kept an eye on the bottom line—but Bobby? Bobby wanted to take over the world, and he was more than willing to use Seth as a means to that end.

Seth was going to get this museum project started because he believed it would be both a great way to extend the Crazy Horse Choppers brand name and also expand their revenue streams. But beyond that, it would showcase the occasional mad genius that was the Boltons. And after that?

After that, Seth was looking toward the future. American-style motorcycles were beginning to take off in popularity in Asia. His uncles and his father—they were family men. All Boltons were. They loved their wives and were actively involved in their children's lives. It would be hard to ask them—even Bobby—to pack up and head to Shanghai for six months or so to open up the Asian market.

But Seth? He was unattached. No wife, no children. Just a restless wanderlust and an up-to-date passport.

That night, after he had pulled Kate on top of him and teased her breasts until she cried out with a shattering orgasm, he lay in the dark, listening to her breathe and feeling her warm body pressed against his. He decided he wouldn't tell her about the possibility of Asia. Not yet, anyway. It was still several months away, and he had to get the museum project going first.

Which meant he had several more months of nights like this.

Twelve

Just like it had every Saturday for the last three weeks, Kate's heart sped up when Seth Bolton walked into Zanger Realty. Today was no exception.

Rain had dampened his hair and a few stray drops clung to his eyelashes, and he was impossibly more handsome now than he'd ever been. When his gaze locked on hers from across the office, she could see how much he'd been waiting for this moment, too.

Because she had been waiting for *him*.

"Ms. Burroughs," he said, his voice going right through her.

"Good morning, Mr. Bolton." It was a little game they played, pretending to be professional when there might be someone else around, even though Harold Zanger rarely came into the office on Saturdays. She stood. "We have a busy day ahead of us—two industrial properties I think will work for you. And after that, are you ready to buy a house?"

He was buying the home on Bitter Root. Her house—although it wasn't hers. Soon, it would be his.

She'd always known she'd be sad when that house sold. But oddly, she was happy that if anyone else had to buy it, it was Seth. He'd take good care of it.

His eyes darkened as his gaze swept over her body. Because he was buying a house today, she had splurged on some new clothes that fit—she'd get her commission before the bills came due. The broomstick skirt with an elastic waist and the tunic top with a deep vee at the neck weren't outright maternity clothes, but she had read that it was a wise financial investment to buy regular clothing one size larger than she had been wearing because she would probably need them after she had the baby.

And although she knew this wasn't a committed relationship, she wanted to look her best for Seth. She couldn't do anything about her rapidly changing body—although Seth seemed to appreciate her new curves far more than she did—but by God she could at least put on flattering clothes. And lingerie. The new lacy black bra—yet another size up—and the matching panties made her feel like she could still be sexy.

Especially when Seth looked at her like that.

"I'm certainly looking forward to celebrating my new home," he said, his voice low. "You look *amazing* today, Kate."

She felt his words—and his desire—in her chest. Everywhere. A shiver went through her—the kind of shiver that promised better things to come. "I've always found home ownership to be *inspiring*." She couldn't wait until the ink was dry on the legal documents and the key to his new house was in his hands. Normally, she would buy clients a gift basket to welcome them to their new home—a candle, a few knickknacks that seemed to match the personalities of the buyers.

Today? She wanted to welcome him to his new home in ways that had nothing to do with candles.

His grin deepened and he took another step into the office, leaving wet footprints on the carpet behind him. "Incredibly inspiring," he agreed. "But assuming the rain moves off, we'll need to make a small side trip."

"Oh?"

His grin tightened and suddenly he looked nervous. "My sister's regular game got delayed because of the storm, but it's supposed to clear off soon. I promised I'd try to stop by. If they win today, they're in the championship."

"This is Julie, right?" They'd talked some about their families, but only enough to scratch the surface. What could she say about her parents?

Her mother was a doormat and her father was a steamroller?

His family life seemed vastly more complicated. The man outright dismissed the notion of living in one place for more than six months at a time and yet he was the most devoted big brother she'd ever met. For a man who wasn't the least interested in setting down roots, he was perfectly happy to spend a crazy amount of money on a luxury home.

After a month of spending time with Seth, she was no closer to understanding him, really.

"Yeah. She and my cousins make up half the starting line. We won't have to stay for the whole game, but I do want to put in an appearance."

She was not looking for anything more permanent. She *wasn't*. She was appreciating this time with Seth as the gift it was. But still, his offer to include her in a family thing warmed her.

Wait a minute. "Will your parents be there?"

He dropped his gaze. "Yeah. The whole family will be."

Oh, dear. Of course, once she had figured out

she would be spending time with Seth, she had looked up the reality show the Boltons had done a number of years ago—even catching glimpses of the teenage Seth working with his father.

Seth had been a cute boy on the verge of manhood then—but the Boltons? Billy was like an angry grizzly bear, Ben Bolton glowered sullenly anytime a camera was shoved in his face, and Bobby? Well, the last Bolton brother wasn't dangerous-looking like his brothers—but he was smooth and sharp and good on camera. And their father? He was the epitome of every tough old biker ever.

And Seth wanted her to meet these people?

"We don't have to," he said into the silence. "They can be overwhelming—trust me, I know."

It was tempting to say that they wouldn't have time for a side trip. Or to say she wasn't dressed for standing in a wet field. Or that she wasn't feeling up to it. All of those would be perfectly fine excuses to save her from meeting the Boltons en masse. Because meeting the whole family—

that felt huge. Far too big for a casual relationship like the one she and Seth had.

But family was forever. Or, for a long time—until they disowned you, anyway. And she'd feel terrible if she caused any sort of trouble for him with his extended family just because she might be a little intimidated by a group of bikers. He was willing to go above and beyond for his family, and she couldn't fault him for that. If anything, she admired him all the more.

So despite her misgivings, she put on a smile and said, "We can do that. But we better get going if we want to have time."

When Seth opened her car door for her, she was past panic and straight over into stark terror. "You're not introducing me as your girlfriend," she told him, staring at his hand. "That's not what this is, right?"

He didn't answer for a long moment, and she suddenly didn't know how he'd answer that question.

Worse, she didn't know how she wanted him to answer that question.

"Right," he finally said, slow and serious. "You're my real estate agent."

Oh, this was a mistake. An epic, huge, grandiose mistake.

But she was going to make it anyway.

After he helped her from the car, they began the long trek to the playing field. Apparently showing up late meant that they got the worst parking spot. Although she'd worn boots to walk around the potential museum sites, she still had to hold her skirt by the hem to keep it from getting wet in the tall grass.

Which was fine because if she was holding her skirt, then she wasn't accidentally holding Seth's hand.

When they reached the playing field, Kate looked around. "Is that them?"

Most of the parents on the sidelines were regular-looking people sitting on folding chairs with coolers. But at the end of the field, there was a group of big, burly men around a cluster of pickup trucks with the tailgates down. The trucks were massive and even at this distance, she could tell they were top-of-the-line.

And the Boltons were *loud*. Kate could hear them bellowing words of encouragement to the players on the field.

"That's them. Don't be intimidated. They're a lot nicer than they look. All bark, no bite—that sort of thing."

She shot him a look.

They paused at midfield, and Seth turned her toward the game. "We're rooting for the green team, the Mustangs. The forward? That's Julie. The right guard's Eliza and the left is Clara— my cousins. They're unbeatable." He said it with obvious pride when any other man his age might have been embarrassed or at least put out to have to give up part of his Saturday on a regular basis to watch little girls kick a ball around. But not him. He really did love his family.

The thought made Kate unexpectedly sad. She hadn't played soccer when she was young—but she'd had dance recitals and choir concerts, and had even acted in a few plays in high school. Her mom had come—but not her dad.

As they watched, Eliza passed the ball to Clara, who faked out a player on the other team and then kicked the ball to Julie, who bounced it off her chest and then kicked it in just past the goalie. The green team erupted into cheers—as did the parents on the sidelines. Especially the group of Boltons at the end of the field. Seth let out a tremendous whoop and the girls on the field pivoted as one and waved at him before their coach bellowed something and they all trotted off down the field.

"They seem pretty good," Kate said as they began to make their way toward his family—and her doom.

No, no—not her doom. Just a really awkward meeting with her not-boyfriend's parents. No need to panic.

"The Mustangs came in second in the championship last year. I think they're going to win it this year. Julie's unstoppable and Eliza is a monster on the field."

Kate kept an eye on the game. Julie and Eliza looked a great deal like each other but Clara? Kate had a feeling that if they all stood still next to each other, she'd be able to see the resemblance, but Clara was much lighter in coloring than the other two.

And then it was too late to turn back because the biggest of the three men stood up from the tailgate and bellowed, "Seth! About damn time. Where the hell have you been?"

Kate recognized him. It was Billy Bolton, the biggest and meanest-looking of the brothers. He was older than he'd been in the reality show, his grizzled beard shot with silver—but he was still a force to be reckoned with.

Then Billy's gaze landed on Kate and she froze like a deer in the headlights.

One of the women—petite and brown and who looked a great deal like Seth—put her hand on Billy's knee. "Language, honey."

A kid about eight or so looked up from the book he was reading. "Seth is here? Yeah!" He hopped up and gave Seth a high five and immediately began telling him about some complicated…card game? Kate couldn't tell.

A little girl, maybe five, squirmed out of Ben Bolton's arms and came charging up to Seth, who caught her easily. "Set!" she crowed. "Spin me!"

Kate's heart clenched at the sight of Seth making a little girl squeal with joy while simultaneously carrying on a very important conversation with a kid. Of course he was great with kids. He was perfect, apparently.

And she was…not.

The woman who'd shushed Billy Bolton stood and made her way over to Kate and instantly, every hair on the back of Kate's neck stood up in warning. "Ignore my husband. Hi, I'm Jenny Bolton. And you are?"

"Kate." Kate swallowed, trying to remember who she was supposed to be right now. But that wasn't easy because every single pair of eyes at this tailgate party were now staring at her. Two other women, both about the same age as Jenny Bolton, closed ranks, standing behind Jenny. "Kate Burroughs," she finally remembered when the one woman with long, dark brown hair raised an eyebrow at her. "Of Zanger Realty. I'm Mr. Bolton's real estate agent."

Someone snorted, but Kate kept her focus on the women. Because it suddenly occurred to her—why had she been worried about the Bolton brothers?

She should have been worried about the Bolton *women*. Including but not limited to the three younger ones running up and down the field.

But maybe not the littlest one. Seth paused in spinning what Kate assumed was another cousin just long enough for the girl to grin at Kate and say, "Your skirt is pretty. Does it twirl?"

"I'm not sure," Kate answered honestly. "Twirling makes me dizzy." And God knew her sense of balance wasn't what it had once been.

"But that's the best part!" The girl giggled and then she and Seth were off again, making big, dizzying circles.

"Real estate?" Jenny's eyes narrowed as she took in everything about Kate. The woman looked too much like Seth not to be his mother.

The woman to Jenny's right was taller, more statuesque, perhaps a little lighter in coloring, but she bore a strong resemblance to Jenny. The woman to Jenny's left, however, had vivid blue eyes and an almost icy demeanor. To a woman, however, they were wearing stunning tops underneath their coats. Kate looked longingly at Jenny Bolton's soft peach sweater. She had a feeling that no matter how much her commission was, she wouldn't be able to afford a sweater like that. The same went for the diamonds in Jenny's ears and around her neck. And that had nothing on what the woman with blue eyes was wearing.

Kate refused to be intimidated by the unified wall of womanhood that was currently looking her up and down. Crap—could these experienced wives and mothers tell she was pregnant? Or were they just judging her by regular feminine standards?

"We were looking at an industrial property not far from here and had time to check in on the game before we signed papers on Mr. Bolton's house this afternoon." All of which was 100 percent the truth and had nothing to do with how good Seth was in bed.

After a moment's hesitation that spoke louder than any niceties could, Jenny said, "I see," in a tone that made it clear that she did—far too well.

Kate swallowed. This was not going well. Feeling desperate, she turned her attention to the rest of the group. "No need to get up," she said when it was obvious no one would, anyway. She gave a little wave. "It's a pleasure to meet you all. I enjoyed your show." Bobby Bolton, still as handsome as ever, grinned—but his brothers both groaned. Kate pressed on. "And I'm excited to help your company move forward into its next venture." There. That was a perfectly professional thing to say.

No one reacted. "Kate's done an amazing job finding the right properties," Seth announced into the awkward silence.

She could feel her face heating up. Somehow, turning tomato red didn't seem to be the reasonable reaction here.

Then it only got worse because in the middle of

that quiet lull, her stomach growled so loudly that it briefly drowned out the sounds of the game. "My apologies," Kate said hastily, wondering if a woman could actually die of embarrassment at a soccer game. "We haven't had time to grab lunch. We should go…"

But the words had no more gotten out of her mouth than the Bolton women descended upon her. "We have food," the paler one said in a surprising British accent. "I'm Stella—Bobby's wife. Clara's mother."

"Besides," the other added, "Connie won't turn loose of Seth for a good twenty minutes and Davey has to talk to someone about Pokémon— all the better if it isn't me. I'm Josey—Ben's wife. The rest of this brood is mine."

"You should sit," Jenny said, moving forward to put a hand on Kate's arm and leading her to a folding chair. "We have chicken or burgers."

And just like that, Kate wasn't on the outside anymore.

She had no idea if that was a good thing or not.

Thirteen

Dimly, Seth was aware that there was still a soccer match going on. But that wasn't the game he was playing right now.

"She's pretty," Bruce Bolton, Seth's grandpa, said. He turned his flinty eyes back to Seth. "What's she doing here with the likes of *you*?"

Seth tried to laugh that off. Over the years, he had learned to hold his own against the Bolton men. But that usually worked best when they'd chosen sides. The Boltons united was a fearsome sight to behold.

Like right now. The three brothers and their

father were all staring at Seth, expecting a reasonable answer. It was at that moment that Seth realized he might have overplayed his hand. Time for some damage control. "Like I said, she's my real estate agent. I'm closing on my house this afternoon." They stared at him like he had lost his ever-loving mind.

"I wouldn't waste my time with a lovely lady like that on real estate," Bruce grumbled. Then he winked at Seth.

"The second site we looked at this morning seems like a good fit for the museum," Seth went on, desperate to keep the conversation away from how pretty Kate was. "It's halfway between the highway and the factory. It costs a little more up front, but the site's already been cleared."

If Seth had had any hope at all that talking shop would distract the Bolton men from the pretty real estate agent currently being coddled by the Bolton women, that hope died on the vine. "You be careful with her," his uncle Ben said.

"I am. I mean," Seth quickly corrected, "it's not like that. We're just working together."

His dad's glare hardened, and Bobby rolled his eyes in disbelief. Even Bruce looked like he wasn't going to buy that line. Seth wasn't a little kid anymore, but he began to sweat it. What if he couldn't convince them there was nothing unbecoming between him and Kate?

The Boltons were family men, and if they thought Seth was leading Kate along under false pretenses, Seth didn't want to even think what they might do. He wouldn't put a shotgun and a preacher past them, though.

But the moment the thought drifted through his brain, something weird happened. Instead of shuddering in horror at the thought, he could see Kate walking toward him, her belly rounded under a simple white dress—not that cupcake confection she'd been wearing the day he'd met her. A smile on her face as she came toward him…

He shook the thought from his head and glanced back over to where his mom and his aunts had surrounded Kate. Jenny had taken a seat next to Kate and appeared to be asking her a series of rapid-fire questions—about what, Seth was afraid to ask. Josey was piling a plate with food and Stella stood back a little ways, watching it all unfold. Kate glanced up and caught his eye. Her cheeks blushed a soft pink before she looked away.

"Yeah," Bobby said, chuckling. "*Just* working together. What did you say her name was?"

"Kate Burroughs."

"And she sells real estate?"

Seth nodded, feeling like he was sixteen and getting busted for staying out past curfew—again.

Bobby's grin turned sharp. "Wasn't there a wedding…?"

Of course Seth should've known that Bobby had his finger on the pulse of Rapid City gossip. "Yeah. I told you guys about that—I found the bride by the side of the road? That's her." He hadn't necessarily wanted to share that particular tidbit of information, but it was better to get out in front of this sort of thing.

Of course, being in front of anything with this

crowd only guaranteed that he'd be run over. "You don't say," Ben said. *"Business."*

Honestly, Seth wasn't sure what this thing with Kate was anymore. It was, in fact, business. But it was also something casual and fun, a rebound to help Kate get back on her feet. And yet...

"Nothing but," he lied.

Not a single one of his male relatives bought that lie. Maybe because Seth didn't buy it himself.

Thankfully, something happened on the playing field and for a moment, everyone's attention focused on the game. The Mustangs were up by three now, with fifteen minutes left in the game. The championship match seemed within their grasp.

He glanced at Kate again. Connie was practically in Kate's lap now, completely enamored of this fancy new person who wore pretty skirts. Kate leaned over, putting her at eye level with Connie. She had a big smile on her face and she clapped when Connie spun for her.

Something in his chest tightened. Kate was

going to be an amazing mother. But he knew how hard it was to be a single parent. He didn't want that for her, damn it all. But aside from throwing two commissions her way, he didn't know how to help.

Kate caught his eye and gave Seth a tight smile. Then, as if by mutual agreement, they both looked away.

When Seth turned his attention back to his family, he found himself squarely in the crosshairs of his father. Billy threw an arm around Seth's shoulders and hauled him off to the side. "You're telling me," Billy began with no other introduction, "that you hired the runaway bride to be your real estate agent on purpose?"

Seth had had his disagreements with his adoptive father over the years. Billy was a hard man who did things his way. He wasn't afraid of a fight, either.

But for all that, he was a remarkably fair man. From the very beginning, he had treated Seth as if he were an equal. Seth wouldn't be half the man he was today if it weren't for his father. And he hated disappointing his father.

But he could tell that Billy was disappointed in him.

"She jilted her fiancé and he kept the house they had together. Her family didn't back her up and she had to quit their real estate office. I'm just helping her out. She needs the commissions."

All of which was true. Or at least, it had been a month ago. Now?

Billy gave him a hard look, one that had Seth standing up straighter. "Women are not to be trifled with, son."

"I am not trifling with her," he defended quickly. He'd made no promises to Kate beyond the next month or so. He was not leading her on with talks of love and marriage. There was no discussion of forever or happily-ever-after. No allusions to a future that existed past the new year. Ergo, it was not trifling.

"We're sending you to Shanghai," his father said in the kind of voice that Seth had seen make grown men damn near wet their pants with terror.

"In the new year. Bobby thinks it could be six, eight months there, with a possibility of Mumbai afterward."

So it'd been decided? Good. Great. He loved it when a plan came together. So why was he filled with a crushing sort of disappointment? "And I'll be ready."

"Does she know that?"

"Of course she does. She knows my job is everything."

His father gave him a long look. "And yet you brought her to your sister's soccer game."

It was not a question. "I don't know how many times I have to say this," Seth ground out, pulling away from his father's embrace. "I'm not leading her on. We have a business relationship. We understand each other perfectly, damn it. And we were in the neighborhood."

Billy was not buying any of this. "If you get her pregnant," he said, as if he were Kate's father instead of Seth's, "your mother and I will expect you to do the right thing."

"I am not going to get her pregnant," Seth retorted. It was impossible to get her pregnant again. "Even if there was something going on between us—which there is not—I would never casually risk her health and well-being and you, of all men, should know that." For a moment, his dad looked almost chastised. Seth forced his shoulders to relax. "Now. Are you done threatening me so we can watch Julie play?"

He expected his father to glower or maybe even yell. So when Billy Bolton cracked a rare smile, Seth was completely caught off guard. "Make sure you're doing the right thing, son," he said, giving Seth a slap on the back that was hard enough to send Seth stumbling. Billy stepped around Seth and went to watch his daughter outplay the other team.

Seth glowered at his father's back. *Of course* he was doing the right thing. He was helping out a single soon-to-be mother. He was ensuring that she would have enough money to live on for the next year, if she wanted to. And he was helping her get over Roger. By the time Seth left for

Shanghai, Kate would be financially secure and ready to move on with her life. Without him.

How was that not the right damn thing?

The garage doors shut behind them, sealing her and Seth off from the rest of the world. The afternoon had passed in a blur of legal documents and signatures, but the end result was now official—the home on Bitter Root was Seth's.

She wasn't going to be sad about that. She was just going to be happy for him, and happy that he was willing to share this home with her, even for a little while.

He opened her car door and held out his hand, just like he always did. "I must say," he said, as she slipped her palm against his and let him help her from the car, "this has been one of the stranger days of my life."

"Buying a home is often very strange," she agreed. But that's not what made today strange for her.

The whole day had been a glimpse into a life she desperately wanted but would never get to have. This house was perfect for her and the family she was going to raise—but she couldn't afford it, not in this life or the next.

Just like Seth's family—aunts and uncles, grandparents and siblings, all coming together for something as mundane as a child's soccer game because they cared. They put family first.

Of course she knew that there were kind, loving, supportive families in the world. And hers was certainly not the worst, by far. But seeing the way that Seth's family had lined up to protect him from an outsider—her? And then there'd been that moment where, apparently by some unspoken agreement, she hadn't been on the outside looking in. She'd been made welcome and fed and, okay, so maybe his mom's questions about Seth's new house had really been thinly veiled questions about Seth and Kate's relationship. But there was no mistaking the fact that Seth's family would do anything for him—for any member of the Bolton family.

She wanted that unconditional love and support

for her child. She wanted that for herself, but she was used to doing without.

Holding her hand, Seth unlocked the garage door. He pulled her inside and then let go long enough to find a light switch. While he did so, she pushed aside her melancholy feelings. There was no point in moping over what she couldn't have. She needed to focus on what she did have— a gorgeous, caring, wealthy man who, for reasons she still didn't fully understand, was more than happy to give her almost everything she wanted.

"Welcome home, Mr. Bolton," she said when he found the light switch. He really was too handsome, she thought when he turned back to her. She tried to strike a sultry pose.

Seth's eyes darkened dangerously. "It's good to be home, Ms. Burroughs." He prowled toward her, the energy that made him so good in bed vibrating off him. "I feel like celebrating. How about you?" He paused, waiting for her answer.

"Yes." Because this was as good as it got. She could make love to Seth in his home and hold on to these happy memories through the long, lonely nights ahead.

He flattened her against the door with his body, hard and hot against hers. But even when he covered her mouth with his, taking and demanding—there was still a gentleness to him.

"Now, Seth," she whispered against his neck, grabbing the belt of his jeans. She didn't want to wait. She didn't want gentle. She just wanted this memory.

"Babe," he growled, and then he picked her up. She squeaked in alarm—she wasn't getting any lighter these days—but Seth cradled her to his chest as if it were the easiest thing in the world. Just like she had from the very beginning, she felt safe in his arms. She knew he wouldn't drop her.

"I apologize for the lack of furniture," he said as he carried her toward the kitchen.

"Don't," she said, throwing her arms around his neck and kissing his jaw. Tucking every contour of his face, every muscle in his neck, away into her memory. "Don't apologize for any of it."

He sat her on the island counter and kissed her

again, harder this time. She managed to get his buckle undone and then he was shoving her flowing skirt up, pulling her panties down. "I need you so much, Kate."

"Yes," she hissed, shoving his pants out of the way. When was the last time anyone had needed her? Roger certainly hadn't. He'd barely even wanted her. Her parents had relied on her because she was cheap labor.

But who needed her because she was Kate?

No one. Just Seth.

They normally took their time with foreplay, but she didn't have the patience for it today and neither did he. He set himself against her and then, with one delicious thrust, buried himself deep inside. Moaning with pleasure, she fell back on her elbows as he grabbed her hips and slammed into her again and again.

She loved being with Seth, but this rawness, this need—this was what had been missing. She had thought he'd been holding himself back out of deference to her being pregnant. But today?

Today, he was like a man possessed. Seth

pounded into her again and again, his finger-tips gripping her hips with brute strength. Kate sprawled on top of the island, surrendering to him completely. Already, she could feel the orgasm spiraling up and up. Pulling her along until her back was arching and she was grabbing at his forearms, desperate for anything to hold on to. When her climax broke, it broke hard, wrenching a guttural cry from her lips. She didn't hold back, either.

She was Kate Burroughs and he needed her.

Seth flung back his head and made a sound that triggered another, smaller shock wave that left Kate completely boneless with satisfaction. He thrust one final time, the cords in his neck strained with the effort.

Then he fell forward, panting hard. She tangled her fingers in his hair and held him to her breast. They hadn't even gotten undressed on the way. It had been the most intense sex of her life, and she was glad it had been with him.

Seth withdrew and pulled her up, crushing her against his chest. Kate could feel the tears running down her face, but this time, it wasn't because the intensity of the orgasm had been overwhelming. She didn't even think it was the hormones, although they weren't helping.

This was supposed to be short-term. Fun. Seth had helped her secure her future. He made her feel desirable and beautiful even though her body was changing constantly. He'd introduced her to his family. And after all of that, he still made passionate love to her.

How was she supposed to let him go?

Fourteen

He could not wait for his bed to show up. An air mattress with two sleeping bags on it wasn't cutting it. Going back to the hotel would have been the smart thing to do. But he hadn't been able to wait to have Kate in this house with him and she was game, so an air mattress it was.

He wanted her in ways that didn't make a whole lot of sense. Which had to be why he was awake at some ungodly hour of the morning, trying to make sense of it all.

Thankfully, Kate was still asleep. She lay curled against his side, her burgeoning belly nestled on his hip, her leg thrown over his. Her breathing was deep and regular, and every so often, she'd twitch a little in her dreams. He hoped they were good dreams.

He gently stroked her hair and tried to think. In the midst of everything that had happened yesterday, Seth had almost overlooked one of the things his dad had said when he'd been telling Seth to man up.

They were sending him to Shanghai in a matter of months, then maybe to India. Which was great. Seth loved to travel. He liked to see the sights and try new foods and…

It wasn't like he had misled Kate. Part of their conversation about him buying a home had revolved around the fact that he was not going to live in it year-round. But he hadn't told her exactly what that entailed.

It was one thing to live in LA for a year. Sure, it took a little while to get from LA to Rapid City and back, but it was doable. Seth had made it home for birthdays and anniversaries and holidays with a few more frequent flyer miles under his belt and a growing distaste for airport coffee.

But Shanghai? Mumbai? Bangkok, maybe? Those weren't quick trips home.

It would be best for everyone, he reasoned, if the break was clean. He did not want to string Kate along. There was probably a great man out there who would appreciate everything she had to offer. Seth wouldn't stand in the way of that by giving her false hope that whenever he made it home, they could pick up where they left off.

Yes, a clean break was best. It just made sense.

Kate stirred against him. "Seth?" Her voice was heavy with sleep. "What's wrong?"

"Nothing," he told her, tightening his grip around her shoulders. "I'm just not used to the air mattress. Go back to sleep."

For a moment, he thought she was going to do just that. After all, he had run her all over God's green earth yesterday—industrial sites, soccer fields, soul-sucking house closings—not to mention several rounds of explosive sex. Plus, she was pregnant and he hadn't missed the yawns she'd hid behind her hands during the signings.

But then she put her palm on his chest and leaned up on her elbow. The room was too dark to see her face, but he knew she was staring down at him. "What aren't you telling me?"

I love you.

The words almost tumbled right off his tongue without his permission. He just managed to get his mouth closed around them before they complicated everything. Because if there was one way to make sure the break wasn't clean, it was those three little words.

"Seth?"

"I'm going to Shanghai," he told her, suddenly glad that they were having this conversation in the dark. He didn't want to see the hurt in her eyes. "My dad confirmed it yesterday at the soccer game."

The silence was heavy. "When?"

"After the holidays." He ran his hand up and down her back, willing her to lie back down. He didn't want to have this conversation about him leaving now. He didn't want to have it ever.

The realization was stunning. He loved her. When the hell had that happened?

"How long will you be gone?" Just because he couldn't see her face didn't mean he couldn't hear the sorrow in her voice. And that cut him deep.

"I'm not sure. At least six months. Probably a year."

"*Oh.*"

Suddenly, he was talking. He couldn't let that one single syllable be the end of this. He couldn't let this be the end.

"I knew this was a possibility, I just thought we might have a few more months. The Boltons are all family men," he explained. "Dad won't leave the shop, anyway. Bobby would go, but he doesn't like to be away from his wife and daughter very long and Stella doesn't like to take Clara out of school. Ben's a homebody and Josey wouldn't leave her school for that long," he explained, desperately trying to make her understand.

"So it has to be you?"

"It's a family business. They made me part of their family." When she didn't reply right away, he added, "I owe them, Kate. You don't know what it was like before they came into my life. Mom and I—we got by okay, but sometimes we were on welfare and in the winter, it got cold. She went to bed hungry so I'd have enough to eat, you know? She tried to hide it from me, always saying she'd eat after I went to bed, but I knew the truth. And I hated that she had to. I *hated* it."

His voice caught in his throat and it took a few moments before he could speak again. Kate didn't rush into the silence, though. She waited.

"I never wanted to see my mom suffer like that. And then, when Billy and Mom got together, that all went away like magic. Suddenly, we had plenty of food and I had my own room and clothes that fit—and I had a dad. I'd never had a dad before." He could still feel the sense of awe he'd felt in court, when the adoption had been finalized. The entire Bolton clan and almost half the reservation had shown up. "I had a *family*."

She sat up, although she didn't take her hand away from his chest. He clutched it, holding her palm over his heart. "I would never ask you to give up your family," she said solemnly. "Not for me."

He rested his hand on her stomach. She had hardly started to show, although now that he had been sleeping with her for a month, he could see the small changes in her body. He was going to give that up, too. He was going to leave before she got to the end of her pregnancy. He wasn't going to be there to see the baby born. He wouldn't see how her body changed with motherhood.

No, he knew that she would never ask. Because that wasn't who she was and that wasn't their deal.

"Kate," he said hoarsely, and then stopped because he couldn't be sure what he was going to say next.

She moved then, straddling him. The faintest glimmer of starlight came in through the bare windows—just enough that he could make out the generous swells of her breasts. His body responded immediately because he couldn't get enough of her.

He might never get enough of her.

She took him into her body and set a slow, steady pace that heated his blood all the same. Nothing stood between them now. "I will miss you," she whispered as he cupped her breasts and teased her nipples. She sank her hands into his hair and pulled him up. "God, how I will miss you."

She shuddered down on him, and he quit trying to fight it. He was lost to her.

What could he offer her? A nice house? Financial stability? Great sex, definitely.

But he couldn't offer her himself. He couldn't be there when she needed him. So instead of telling her that he loved her, that she was everything, he forced himself to say, "I will, too, babe," because it was the truth—just not the one he wanted it to be.

"So this is it, then?" Seth asked as he looked over Bobby Bolton's expansion plans for Shanghai.

"This is it," Bobby said, lounging in the chair

in front of Seth's desk. "Setting up the showroom in Shanghai, training the staff, making sure everything goes smoothly for the Asia launch. In a perfect world, it'll take you six months."

"The world ain't perfect," Seth said, the sour feeling settling in his stomach. He didn't speak Chinese. He wasn't fluent in the local power structures. He needed to figure out his target market and the best way to reach them.

Even assuming he found the right bilingual staff who understood motorcycles, Seth was looking at a year in China.

He had jumped at the chance to go to LA for a year. He loved his family, but there was no getting around the fact that the Boltons could be overwhelming. And even then, Bobby had made a habit of stopping in every few months, unannounced, to see how things were going.

China was the ultimate fresh start. Seth should've been thrilled by this prospect.

"You know," Bobby said in a kind of voice that Seth had long since recognized as manipulative, "we could send someone else. I've made a few contacts…"

"What? No—I'm going. I'm a partner in this company. This is my job." He was a Bolton. He worked for the family business. He wasn't about to shirk his duties because he'd accidentally fallen in love with Kate.

The sour feeling in his stomach got more awful.

"The museum project is barely off the ground," Bobby went on, as if Seth hadn't spoken. "We still need to select the architect, finalize the design, and then there's the actual building to oversee."

"You're going to handle that." Of all the brothers, Bobby was the one who traveled the most—and that wasn't just because his wife was British. But the man practically turned into a homebody from September to May while Clara was in school.

Bobby stared at him flatly. Seth heard himself continue, "This was the deal, man. I promised to do this and I'm not going to go back on my promises to you guys. We're family." Bobby didn't respond, and an odd sort of dread churned around with the sourness. "Aren't we?"

"Have you ever spoken with your dad?" Bobby asked unexpectedly.

What the hell kind of question was that? "I talked to him this morning when I came into work. Why?"

"No, I mean your birth father. Have you ever talked to him?"

It shouldn't have hit Seth like a sledgehammer to the chest—but it did. "No. I don't even know who he was. All I know is that he left. Mom was pregnant and he left her alone."

He did not like the way Bobby was looking at him. The man was perhaps the most intelligent of the three brothers, but he hid it behind a veneer of playboy charm. There was no getting around the fact that Bobby played a long game. "She's pregnant, isn't she?"

The hits just kept on coming. "I'm not the father."

There was no need to ask who had figured it out. Kate had come to Julie's championship game—the Mustangs had easily won. And if no one had asked her if she was expecting, that was because her body made that question irrelevant. She was soft and round and glowing. Any idiot could see that she was with child—and his family was not full of idiots.

However, no one had asked. Kate's impending joy had been the elephant in the room that they had all avoided talking about at the game and ever since. Even Billy had skirted the subject, instead favoring Seth with hard looks that said more than words ever would.

Now Seth was going to leave Kate behind. Because his first priority was his family. Because that was what Boltons did. Family was first. Family was everything.

And Kate was...

He was going to be sick.

"I made a promise to you guys and to the company," Seth said slowly. "I haven't made any promises to anyone else." Which was true.

So why did saying it feel like a betrayal?

Because Kate was spending almost every night

in Seth's bed and every morning in his arms. Because they ate dinner together and talked about their days.

Because he had asked her if she wanted him to go with her to her doctor's appointment where she found out she was having a girl. He'd discussed names with her. Because he had a diamond solitaire pendant with matching earrings already wrapped in silver-and-red paper with her name on it—his parting gift to her before he left.

Because, like an idiot, he had completely fallen in love with her. Deeply, irrevocably in love.

It didn't help that Bobby was still staring at him. Usually, you couldn't shut the man up. But today, he was acting more like Billy than ever. "Who else does she have? I did some digging, you know. Her ex-fiancé stayed with her parents' firm. An old friend had to give her a job. And then a certain knight in shining armor rode in and threw some big commissions her way. But if you leave, who else will she have?"

It was not uncommon for the Bolton brothers to come to blows. Bobby and Billy were like oil and water, and although Ben did his best to keep them from pummeling each other, Seth had seen a few noses get busted in his time.

Aside from that one incident before his parents had gotten married, Seth had never been a part of a family brawl. Mostly because he wasn't nearly as big as his dad and his uncles, but also it didn't seem right to take on the men who'd made a place for him.

But right now? Right now, he wanted to break Bobby's jaw. And maybe a few other bones, just for good measure. "If you're going to say something, just say it."

Bobby cracked that smooth grin of his. Seth wanted to push it in with his fist. "Wouldn't be surprised in the least if your aunts didn't descend upon that poor woman. Your mom, especially, wouldn't like the idea of Kate being all alone when she has that baby."

No, of course Mom wouldn't. Even though Seth was twenty-five years old now. Even though Mom had been married to Billy for almost eleven years, Jenny Bolton still ran an after-school support group for pregnant teenagers because she didn't want anyone to feel as alone as she had when she'd been pregnant with Seth.

"Are you done yet?" Seth ground out. "Because I don't know what you want me to do here, Bobby. You show up with a plan that will have me in Shanghai for almost a year and then simultaneously make me feel like crap for doing my job? Go to hell. And get out of my office." It felt damn good to be able to say that.

Bobby stood, in no hurry to go anywhere. He straightened his cuffs and popped his neck from side to side. "I'm not the one making you feel bad, kid." He headed for the door, but paused with his hand on the knob. "And we *are* family, Seth. Family is the most important thing we have." The words settled in the room like silt at the bottom of standing water.

Seth understood what Bobby was saying. His uncle had just been playing devil's advocate— but they still expected him to put the family first and do his best to open up the Asian market. "I understand."

He was definitely going to be sick.

Bobby gave him a measured look. "Do you?"

And with that parting shot, he was gone.

Fifteen

"Katie, my girl," Harold Zanger said, striding out of his office and snapping his suspenders. "How are you getting on this fine day?"

Kate patted her ever-growing stomach. "Fine," she said with a smile as Harold beamed. She left out the part where she had to pee every seven minutes and her back hurt. According to the doctor, things were going perfectly. She only had another three months to go.

"Is that Mr. Bolton of yours going to be coming around?" Harold asked the question in a too-casual manner.

But Kate didn't miss the *yours* in that question. "I don't think it's physically possible for him to buy any more real estate," she said, dodging the question.

Seth was not hers. In fact, with Christmas weeks away, he was less hers every single day.

They hadn't talked about it, but she knew he was leaving soon. And she knew it was selfish, but she didn't want him to go. The last three months with him had been the best three months of her life.

Harold gave her a kindly look. "He's done all right by you, hasn't he?"

Kate looked away. "He has. But then," she said, forcing a smile to her lips, "so have you."

Harold patted her on the shoulder. "You're a sweet girl, Katie. You deserve better." Tears stung in her eyes as Harold gave her shoulder a squeeze and then turned away, politely pretending she wasn't about to cry. "I'm off to show some houses today," he announced loudly, giving his suspenders another snap just for good measure. "You'll hold down the fort?"

"Of course," she said, smiling through it all.

Seth had done right by her. Thanks to the purchase of the house—which still had next to no furniture in it—and the industrial property, she was able to plan to take six months off with her little girl, whom she'd decided to name Madeleine.

More than that, he had given her back her sexuality. Kate hadn't even realized what she'd been missing until Seth had come into her life. But now? She wouldn't settle for anything less. He had built her up instead of wearing her down, and never again would she go along just to get along.

Seth was leaving and she was going to let him go. It would be selfish to hold him here, but God, she was going to miss the hell out of him.

She was lost in these thoughts and others— what should she get him for Christmas?—when the chimes over the door jingled. "It's a zinger of a day at Zanger, how may I…" She looked up to see a familiar figure standing in the doorway.

Her stomach curdled because she recognized that man—and it wasn't Seth.

"Roger?" What the hell was he doing here?

He looked like hell. Oh, he still looked good. His hair was combed, his face cleanly shaven, his suit nicely pressed. But as he stepped into the office, Kate could see the shadows under his bloodshot eyes. He looked like he hadn't slept in a week, maybe longer. "Kate," he said, and then stopped when she stood up. His eyes widened. "God, you look so…"

She didn't know if it was anger or adrenaline—she hadn't seen him in months. Not since he'd agreed to pay child support but promised that he'd never have anything to do with her daughter. "Pregnant?" she finished before he could say something crass. "Yes. I'm pregnant. I told you that, remember?"

He didn't even have the decency to look ashamed at coming within a hairbreadth of insulting her. "Yeah, I know. I just didn't…" He waved a hand in her general direction.

She blinked at him. "If you're implying that I was lying about being pregnant—"

"No, no. I believe you. You just look…"

How had she ever thought she could love this man? It'd been a crappy lie that she had forced herself to buy into because, for some reason she still didn't understand, her dad liked this man. Maybe it was because Roger and her father were too much alike. And Kate did exactly what her mother had done—shut up and went along with what her father wanted.

Well, no more. Seth had spent months telling her how gorgeous she was, how beautiful she looked—even as she got huge. She was carrying Roger's daughter and all he could think about was that she'd gotten fat.

He could go to hell.

"Did you have a reason for being here or did you just feel like insulting the mother of your unborn child?"

Roger recoiled.

"And I swear to God, Roger, if you ask if I'm

sure it's your child, I will not be held responsible for my actions."

"Jeez, Kate—calm down. I didn't come here to pick a fight."

When, in the history of womankind, had telling a woman to "calm down" ever worked? Because it sure as hell didn't now. "Then why are you here?"

He scrubbed at the back of his neck. "Listen, I've been thinking—that kid's not even born yet. You're not going to need any child support for what, another year or so?"

Good Lord, just when she thought it couldn't get any worse, it did. "What are you talking about?"

"I heard you had a few big sales," he went on, completely missing the horrified shock in her voice. "To Bolton, of all people. I would've thought he'd come to me if he needed something—we're friends."

Liar, Kate thought. She'd been spending nearly every waking moment with Seth for the last several months and not once had Roger made an effort to talk to either of them.

She didn't say that, though. Instead, she focused on what Roger was really saying. "Yes, I sold some property. I happen to be a real estate agent. What's it to you?"

"You don't have to get all upset," he said, his eyes darting around the office. "I'm just saying, it would probably be best if we delayed the child support payments for a little while. That's all."

"Best for who?" Roger tried to smile, but it was more of a grimace. "Roger, what the hell is going on? I'm pregnant and you rolled in here to insult my appearance and try to get out of your financial obligations to a child you helped create?"

"Hey, I didn't ask you to get pregnant."

"News flash, I didn't ask to get pregnant. It was an accident, but if you're going to act like I did this all by myself, I'm going to have to explain some basic biology to you. What do you want?"

The silence was awkward, but she debated whether or not she needed backup. How fast could Seth get here?

"See," Roger began, and she heard the whine in his voice that made it clear that he hadn't gotten his way with something, "there were some investments that didn't pan out and business has been slow and…"

"And you're suddenly broke?" she supplied.

"*Broke* is a strong word. But there have been some cash flow difficulties."

She mentally translated those passive statements. Why hadn't she ever noticed that when Roger screwed up he never owned his mistakes? "You lost all your money, didn't you? What's the matter, my dad cut you off?"

That grimace again. Roger looked like a cornered animal trying to bluff its way out of a dangerous situation. "Look, are you going to help me out or not?"

The nerve of this man. And to think, she might've been stuck with him. "You want me to help you out by releasing you from your financial obligations to your own child for an indeterminate amount of time because you made some unwise investment choices and you don't have me to bail you out—am I getting all of this right?"

Finally, he looked ashamed of himself. As well he should. "I wouldn't put it quite like that. We could get married, you know."

She almost gagged. "No," she said with as much force as she could. "I don't have to take your crap, Roger. I don't love you. You never loved me. And if you try to bail on child support, I will sue you back to the Stone Age."

"Come on, Kate—"

"No," she repeated again. "You kept the house. You kept the wedding gifts. You went on the honeymoon without me. What do I get? Child support. I had to rely on a family friend to give me a job. You gave me nothing, Roger. You are legally obligated to provide for your child. And I will hold you to it. There's nothing else I want from you."

He jerked as if she had slapped him. "When did you get so bitchy?"

Oh, that just did it. "Get out. I'm not your doormat anymore."

"But—"

"Now," she repeated, putting as much menace as she could into her voice.

The jerk had the nerve to just stand there and stare, his mouth open in shock.

She was reaching for her phone when the door behind him jingled and suddenly, there was Seth Bolton, stepping around Roger and putting himself in between that jerk and Kate. "Roger," he said, his voice cool. He looked back at Kate. "Everything okay here?"

"Yes," Kate said before Roger could attempt to turn on the charm—not that Seth would fall for it. "Roger was just leaving, after renewing his commitment to paying child support." She left the *or else* hanging invisibly in the air.

Roger was an idiot, but not such a great idiot that he was going to argue with her in front of an audience. "We can talk later," he said in a conciliatory tone.

"No," she said, standing up as straight as her belly would allow. "We can't."

"Let me see you out," Seth said, almost—but

not quite—sounding friendly. He crowded Roger toward the door and opened it, waiting.

Roger's shoulders slumped in defeat. He looked back at Kate and said, "You look great, you know."

There was a time when Kate would have clung to that halfhearted compliment as proof that Roger did care for her, that she was doing the right thing staying with him. Now?

Too little, too late. She did not return the compliment.

Roger opened his mouth as if he were going to say something else, but Seth cleared his throat. It was the most menacing sound Kate had heard come out of him yet.

Then the men were outside and Kate half wanted Seth to take a swing at Roger and half just wanted the idiot to go away.

She was going to have to take Roger to court— that much was obvious. Lawyers were going to be expensive, but she wasn't going to let him weasel his way out of this.

She sank down in her desk chair and dropped

her head into her hands. He hadn't even asked if she was going to have a boy or girl. Why was she surprised? She wasn't, really. Of course Roger was going to disappoint her. He really didn't care. Not about the baby, not about her.

The door jingled again and there was Seth, shutting it firmly behind him. "He's gone," he said, looking at her with open concern. "Are you all right?"

Kate's throat was thick with emotion—damned hormones. "I stood up to him," she said around the lump in her throat. "He doesn't want to pay child support and I told him I'd sue him if I had to. God, what a hassle."

Seth grinned at that. He glanced back at Harold's dark office and then came around her desk, pulling her up into his arms. "You were amazing," he agreed. Rubbing her back in just the right place. "I wish I could've seen the whole thing."

She was crying—but she was also laughing. "Oh, you would've hit him. I would've liked to have seen that." Seth leaned back and stroked her tears away. She loved that her random bouts of hormones didn't freak him out. "I can't believe I almost married him."

He cradled her face. "I'm so glad you didn't."

Kate almost lost herself in the tenderness of the moment. No—she couldn't fall for Seth all over again. "Did he say anything to you outside?"

Seth snorted. "He seemed hurt that I hadn't used him for my real estate agent."

"Lord."

Seth hugged her tighter, and she sank into his warmth. He was always here when she needed him, lending her his strength. Without him, she might have buckled and agreed to marry Roger. She might have let Roger out of his financial obligations.

She would've been miserable. But she wasn't. Upset, yes. Pregnant, definitely. But she'd refused to roll over to make someone else happy. Seth had shown her she could fight for what she wanted and for that, she would love him forever.

He stepped all the way around her and began to knead his thumbs into her lower back. God, it felt so good. "What are you doing here?"

"I needed to see you," he said, sending a thrill through her. Then, after a long pause while he worked on a particularly sore spot, he added, "We finalized the plan for the Shanghai showroom."

All of her good feelings disappeared in a heartbeat. Because this was it—the end. "Oh?" she got out in a strangled-sounding voice.

"Yeah." Kate couldn't tell if it was a consolation or not that he sounded almost as depressed as she felt. "Best-case scenario is Shanghai for six months, but it'll probably be closer to ten, maybe even twelve."

She shut her eyes, although that didn't change things. "That's great," she lied, because his job was important to him. His family was important to him, and she could not allow him to damage those relationships for her.

"Yeah," he said again, sounding positively morose about it. "It's going to be really exciting. I'll leave on the second."

They were down to days at this point. Sixteen days. And then he would be gone from her life and she would still be here, arguing with Roger and trying to do the best she could with what she had.

Suddenly, she couldn't bear it. She turned, throwing her arms around his neck. "I wish I could go with you."

His hands cradled her belly. "I couldn't ask it of you. I wish I could stay."

She shook her head against his shoulder. "I couldn't ask it of you, either."

He pulled a small box out of his pocket. "I got this for you."

She stared at the Christmas wrapping. She didn't want to open it—didn't want to accept the fact that the best thing that had ever happened to her was winding down to its natural conclusion. "Thank you. I haven't had time to get you a present yet."

"I don't…" He pulled her back into his arms and held her for a long moment. Then, almost by unspoken agreement, they both pulled back. Lingering would do no one any good. "Promise me," he said, taking her hands and staring down into her eyes. "Promise me you'll take care of yourself and Madeleine. Promise me you won't…" He swallowed, his eyes suspiciously bright. "Don't wait for me, Kate. There's a great guy out there who is going to be really lucky to have you and I don't want you to pass him up."

"You're being ridiculous," she said, hiccupping. She was almost seven months pregnant. The number of men who would look at her and see anything but baggage could probably be counted on one hand.

In fact, there might only be one of them. Standing right in front of her.

"If you need anything," he went on, ridiculous or not, "you call my parents. My mom's an expert about single moms with new babies. Okay?"

"Seth—"

"Promise me, Kate," he insisted, squeezing her hands.

All good things came to an end. And that was what this was. The end. "I promise."

She'd never realized how much that sounded like goodbye.

Sixteen

An odd sort of tension settled in and made itself comfortable between Seth and his family. Sure, they all opened presents together Christmas morning. But even Julie, who professed to still believing in Santa Claus, was giving him looks that he didn't want to think about. She was too much like their father sometimes, and he was in no mood to be judged by a ten-year-old.

His mom would look at him and sigh and damned if it didn't sound like disappointment. And his dad? The temperature dropped a solid ten degrees anytime he walked into the room.

No one spoke about it. No one asked about Kate. They barely talked about Shanghai. Just tension.

Just Seth slowly going insane. He hadn't seen her since that day in her office—the day he'd given her the necklace. She hadn't opened it. He almost called her Christmas afternoon but he told himself he'd wanted a clean break and that it was for the best.

That didn't explain why he called Kate on New Year's Eve and asked her to come spend it with him. She must have been doing okay, because she refused and in a way, he was glad. He was flying out first thing on the second to LA and from there, to mainland China. If she came over for one last night, he honestly had no idea how he was going to leave.

He was miserable and pissy and worried sick about her being alone for Madeleine's birth. Even though he knew that if the shit hit the fan his family would step up and make sure Kate was taken care of, he still worried. What if Roger came back? What if she had to sue him for child support? What if there was a problem with Madeleine? Hell, what if there wasn't? He remembered how hard it'd been for everyone the first few months after Julie had been born. And Julie had had Mom, Dad and Seth to take care of her. How would Kate handle the sleepless nights and diapers and feedings by herself?

He did his best not to worry as he packed up his stuff. His dad took him to the airport. It was still pitch-black at five in the morning, but at least it was clear. Flying out of South Dakota in the middle of winter was always dicey.

True to form, they didn't talk. Billy just glowered, and Seth? He tried to focus on the future. He'd never been one to settle down. Wandering all over God's green earth was who he was. He knew it. Kate knew it. His family knew it.

At least, he thought they did. They got to the airport and Billy silently helped unload Seth's bags and Seth couldn't remember ever having been more miserable than he was right now because this felt wrong. Everything about it was wrong.

Panicking hard, Seth stood before the only man he'd ever called father. "I'm not Madeleine's father," he said, wishing he could take the words back even before he was done saying them.

It was not Dad's business—it was none of anyone's business. But he knew, deep down inside, that Billy Bolton was disappointed in him.

Billy jammed his hands on his hips and stared up at the midnight-black sky. "No, I didn't figure you were."

"I have to put the family first."

Once, long ago, Seth had punched this man in the face for daring to break up with his mom. It was the only time he'd ever struck Billy, and the man hadn't yelled or hit back. Instead, he'd looked at Seth with disappointment in his eyes— the same disappointment in his eyes right now. "Neither of them is family, but you already know that baby's name."

Seth's throat closed up. "You guys made me a Bolton. That wasn't something I took lightly. I'm not going to let you or the business down."

Seth hadn't realized he was staring at the sidewalk until Billy's massive hands settled on Seth's shoulders. "Son," he said, and it just about broke Seth's heart to hear that word spoken with so much sadness, "God knows I tried to do right by you and your mom. And God knows if it weren't for motorcycles, I'd either be dead or in jail."

"I know," Seth said, wishing for numbness because he couldn't take this. The business kept his father going and he couldn't turn his back on that.

Billy's grip on him tightened. "Look at me, Seth." Seth raised his head, swallowing back tears. "The business is important, but we could lose it tomorrow and it wouldn't change anything about you and me and our family. We will always be family because we chose you, and more important, you chose us." He gave Seth a little shake. "You don't have to prove a damned thing to me. You never did."

Then he pulled Seth into a mammoth bear hug before quickly shoving him away. "Write your mother," he called out as he got back into his truck and drove off.

Seth stood there for a moment in the freezing air, shaking.

He hadn't chosen the Boltons—his mom had. His aunt had—they'd both married brothers. He'd been part of the deal, but not as a voting member. He'd just…

He'd spent the last ten years of his life living and breathing motorcycles and the motorcycle business because when he welded a frame Billy approved of or pitched an idea Bobby got behind, it made Seth feel like he was part of something. Crazy Horse Choppers had given him a place. A purpose.

That was what mattered.

Wasn't it?

Not that anyone was buying real estate right now—no one really wanted to move on the second day of the year in the middle of winter—but Kate went to work anyway. She couldn't handle staying alone in her crappy apartment all day, staring at the lovely Christmas card her mother had sent.

She wore the stunning diamond pendant necklace and matching earrings Seth had bought for her. She wasn't an expert in diamonds, but she'd listened when the jewelry salespeople had talked cut and clarity and all that and she was wearing probably close to four carats of diamonds. It wasn't a stretch to say that she was wearing close to fifty thousand dollars' worth of jewelry—a fortune.

He'd spent that on her. It was a hell of a farewell gift and, if worse came to worst, it would take care of her and Madeleine for a long time.

But she couldn't bear the thought of selling Seth's gifts. She'd sold her engagement ring because she hadn't wanted to hang on to another reminder of Roger—and she'd needed the cash. But Seth's pendant?

She wore it on a long chain so it nestled next to her heart. It was the only way she could keep him close.

That, and being here at work. There were so many memories of Seth here. Hearing the door jingle and looking up to see Seth standing there, that grin on his face. She didn't want to entirely leave those memories right now, either. It was easier to pull those memories around her like a blanket at the office. She was even gladder that she'd never had him over to her apartment. It would've been too much.

She glanced at the clock—again—and slid the diamond along the chain. Seth should've landed in LA by now. He was probably holed up in a bar, waiting for his flight to China. Was he thinking of her? Was he wishing that she'd taken him up on his offer to ring in the New Year—just one more night together? She'd known she needed to say no to him, but now she wished she'd said yes. Because it already sucked, letting him go. What would one more night have hurt?

The baby fluttered in her stomach, and Kate put her hand to where Madeleine was kicking. This was what she had to focus on now—impending motherhood. For all intents and purposes, she was all Madeleine had.

No, it wasn't exactly true. Seth had made her swear that if she needed any help, she'd contact his family. Part of Kate knew that wasn't a good idea because, while she genuinely liked his parents and his sister, that would presume a relationship that otherwise no longer existed.

On the other hand, it was clear from her mother's Christmas card that there wouldn't be a close relationship with her parents. And Kate was just coming to grips with the fact that she had a long, cold, dark three months of being extremely pregnant ahead of her.

It wouldn't be so bad if Madeleine were already here. The baby was going to take every little bit of energy Kate had—and probably some she didn't have. She wouldn't be able to dwell on Seth's absence once Madeleine arrived.

Kate tried diligently to focus on listings. The family she'd spoken to a few months ago was being relocated to Rapid City and anticipated moving by March. And since Kate had recently been in a vast majority of the homes currently on the market, she could with great confidence eliminate most of them.

That was what she was supposed to be thinking

about. But even in that, her thoughts turned back to Seth. He'd purchased the house that she had long wanted—but refused to furnish it without her input. The house could be such a showplace, but right now, it was little more than an exaggerated bachelor pad, stacked with boxes that had been in storage. She hoped Seth would hire a good interior decorator when he came home and make something out of that house.

She was making another cup of tea in the small kitchen tucked behind Harold's office when the door jingled. "It's a zinger of a day here at Zanger," she called over her shoulder, pouring the hot water over the tea bag. Who knew? Someone had actually come looking for a house. It was a good thing she was here. "I'll be right with you."

She walked out into the main part of the office and then pulled up short so quickly that water splashed all over the place.

She was hallucinating, because it wasn't possible that Seth was here.

Then he smiled and she realized that no, she

couldn't be imagining this. Seth Bolton himself stood in the doorway of the office.

He'd come for her.

He couldn't have come for her.

"Seth? What are you doing here?"

His smile faltered a little. "I've been thinking," he said, taking a hesitant step into the office.

"But… You are supposed to be on a plane? Or in LA by now. You're not supposed to be here."

"I couldn't leave," he said, his voice hoarse. "I couldn't leave you."

The room started to swim and the next thing she knew, she was in Seth's arms and he was lowering her down into her chair. "Breathe, babe," he said, kneeling in front of her and holding her hands.

"You're not supposed to give up your job with the company for me," she said, her voice cracking. "I would never ask you to put me before your family."

"You're not asking," he said, stroking his thumbs over the back of her hands. "Kate, I screwed up. I want to make it right and then, if you still want to be done, I'll go."

He'd come back for her. She didn't want him to leave again. She wasn't sure she was strong enough for that.

"We had an agreement," she said weakly. "Fun. No strings. You're not going to stay in Rapid City. That was the deal."

"I want to renegotiate the deal. I'm looking for something fun. Some strings attached. Slightly more permanently based in Rapid City. At least until Madeleine is old enough to travel."

At that moment, the baby chose to shift, sending flutters all over Kate's belly. Seth cupped her stomach and leaned down to kiss it through her clothes.

"You can't mean this," she said, giving up the fight against the tears. What was it about this man that always had her at her weakest?

He looked up at her, so handsome and perfect and *here*. "I never knew my father. He ran out on my mom before I was even born and I thought... I thought I was restless. That I needed to see the world—and that was because of him. But I don't think I'm restless. I just think I hadn't found a reason to stay in one place."

"Don't say that," she begged. "Don't break my heart, Seth. I can't take it."

"I couldn't take it, either—so I won't."

"I won't let you do this. I will not let you give up the family business for me. I'm not…"

His gaze sharpened. "You *are* worth it, Kate. And you know what? I'm a Bolton and if there's one thing I know about Boltons, it's that family is everything. Kate, you are *my* everything. What kind of man would I be if I didn't fight for you?"

She threw her arms around his neck and buried her face against his cheek. "No one has ever fought for me before," she wept. "I just don't want you to regret it."

"Have a little faith in me," he said, his voice shaking. "And have faith in yourself. Do you love me?"

"Of course I do," she sobbed. "How could I not?"

"Then marry me, Kate. And not in some big

lavish ceremony with a crazy dress that has petticoats and corsets and ruffles and strings. We
can get married at the courthouse, for all I care.
It's not the wedding that counts—it's you. You're
my everything, Kate, you and Madeleine. Let
me be your family. It doesn't mean I won't do
stupid things like nearly flying halfway across
the world when I belong right here. That means
I will fight for you, for us. Every day of my life,
so help me God."

"But your job…"

He leaned back and gave her a cocky look. "I'm
a partner in the firm. It's not like they can fire
me. And besides, it'll work out. It might be a little
messy, but I'll fight for what I want. I don't have
to prove myself to them. I just have to prove myself to you." He swallowed. "If you'll have me?"

"Yes," she said, pulling him into a kiss. "God,
yes, Seth. I couldn't even think with you being
gone."

The baby shifted again, harder this time—
demanding attention, no doubt. Kate gasped as
Seth rubbed her belly. "I couldn't miss this. She

will always be my daughter, from the very first moment."

This was everything she'd ever wanted. She wasn't perfect, not by a long shot—but Seth understood who she was and loved her anyway. She cupped his cheek with her hand. "Seth?"

"Yeah?" He turned his head and pressed a kiss against her palm.

"You were right."

His eyes darkened as she ran her hands through his hair. "Oh? About what?"

"You're good for me," she replied, leaning forward to brush her lips against his. "Very, very good for me."

He grinned against her mouth. "Babe," he all but growled, pulling her into his embrace, "I'm just getting started."

Epilogue

"You don't think she'll run, do you?"

Seth shot Bobby a dirty look as the judge cleared his throat. "Shall we begin?"

Jack Roy began to strum his guitar as Julie walked into the judge's chambers, strewing rose petals before her. Davey walked next to his cousin, intensely focused on the rings he was carrying. Clara, Eliza and Connie giggled while their mothers shushed them.

Billy smacked Bobby on the arm and Ben made a noise of warning deep in his throat. Seth ignored them all because just then, Kate walked through the double doors, holding a sleeping Madeleine in her arms instead of a bouquet.

Seth's heart clenched at the sight of his family. Not that he hadn't seen them this morning—he'd gotten up with Madeleine at two so Kate could sleep.

But his aunt Stella had worked her magic, designing a simple cream wedding gown that clung to Kate's ample chest and flowed softly away from the waist. Compared to the monstrosity that Kate had almost gotten married in the first time, Seth was thrilled to realize this dress wouldn't require three lady's maids to remove.

Madeleine wore a similar outfit, although her fabric had been dyed with the faintest pink. Seth couldn't see his daughter's feet because the dress flowed well past Madeleine's legs.

"Beautiful," Billy whispered, sounding almost wheezy about it.

"Mine," Seth replied.

"I'm proud of you, son," Billy went on, his voice low enough that no one else could hear him. "I knew you'd do the right thing."

The last six months had been a whirlwind of change. Kate had moved into their home and Seth had given her free rein to decorate it as she saw fit. Madeleine had come two weeks early, healthy and beautiful. Seth had been with Kate for the entire twenty-two hours of labor.

He'd personally hired a man he'd worked with in LA who, it turned out, spoke semi-fluent Mandarin to spearhead the Shanghai showroom.

And Seth? He'd stayed in Rapid City, overseeing the museum expansion.

Expanding his family.

Today, not only would Kate become his wife, but Madeleine would legally be his daughter. He and Kate had debated getting hitched immediately—Seth's preference—but Kate had decided she wanted to wait until Madeleine could be a part of the ceremony.

Seth caught the eye of his future in-laws. Kate's dad was scowling, but he'd put on a boutonniere and he was here, so that was something. Kate's mom was dabbing at her eyes. Seth hoped that for Kate's sake, they could have a cordial relationship, if not a close one.

Then Seth turned his attention back to his bride.

The judge, it turned out, was an old riding buddy of Billy's. He'd been happy to combine a wedding and an adoption.

Kate made her way up to Seth and handed Madeleine off to Jenny. Then, before their families, God and the state of South Dakota, he married his bride and adopted his daughter.

He was a Bolton and this was his family. By God, he would do anything for them. They were the right thing. They always would be.

* * * * *

MILLS & BOON®
Hardback – September 2017

ROMANCE

The Tycoon's Outrageous Proposal	Miranda Lee
Cipriani's Innocent Captive	Cathy Williams
Claiming His One-Night Baby	Michelle Smart
At the Ruthless Billionaire's Command	Carole Mortimer
Engaged for Her Enemy's Heir	Kate Hewitt
His Drakon Runaway Bride	Tara Pammi
The Throne He Must Take	Chantelle Shaw
The Italian's Virgin Acquisition	Michelle Conder
A Proposal from the Crown Prince	Jessica Gilmore
Sarah and the Secret Sheikh	Michelle Douglas
Conveniently Engaged to the Boss	Ellie Darkins
Her New York Billionaire	Andrea Bolter
The Doctor's Forbidden Temptation	Tina Beckett
From Passion to Pregnancy	Tina Beckett
The Midwife's Longed-For Baby	Caroline Anderson
One Night That Changed Her Life	Emily Forbes
The Prince's Cinderella Bride	Amalie Berlin
Bride for the Single Dad	Jennifer Taylor
A Family for the Billionaire	Dani Wade
Taking Home the Tycoon	Catherine Mann

0817 GEN STD HB

MILLS & BOON®
Large Print – September 2017

ROMANCE

The Sheikh's Bought Wife	Sharon Kendrick
The Innocent's Shameful Secret	Sara Craven
The Magnate's Tempestuous Marriage	Miranda Lee
The Forced Bride of Alazar	Kate Hewitt
Bound by the Sultan's Baby	Carol Marinelli
Blackmailed Down the Aisle	Louise Fuller
Di Marcello's Secret Son	Rachael Thomas
Conveniently Wed to the Greek	Kandy Shepherd
His Shy Cinderella	Kate Hardy
Falling for the Rebel Princess	Ellie Darkins
Claimed by the Wealthy Magnate	Nina Milne

HISTORICAL

The Secret Marriage Pact	Georgie Lee
A Warriner to Protect Her	Virginia Heath
Claiming His Defiant Miss	Bronwyn Scott
Rumours at Court (Rumors at Court)	Blythe Gifford
The Duke's Unexpected Bride	Lara Temple

MEDICAL

Their Secret Royal Baby	Carol Marinelli
Her Hot Highland Doc	Annie O'Neil
His Pregnant Royal Bride	Amy Ruttan
Baby Surprise for the Doctor Prince	Robin Gianna
Resisting Her Army Doc Rival	Sue MacKay
A Month to Marry the Midwife	Fiona McArthur

0817 GEN STD LP

MILLS & BOON®
Hardback – October 2017

ROMANCE

Claimed for the Leonelli Legacy	Lynne Graham
The Italian's Pregnant Prisoner	Maisey Yates
Buying His Bride of Convenience	Michelle Smart
The Tycoon's Marriage Deal	Melanie Milburne
Undone by the Billionaire Duke	Caitlin Crews
His Majesty's Temporary Bride	Annie West
Bound by the Millionaire's Ring	Dani Collins
The Virgin's Shock Baby	Heidi Rice
Whisked Away by Her Sicilian Boss	Rebecca Winters
The Sheikh's Pregnant Bride	Jessica Gilmore
A Proposal from the Italian Count	Lucy Gordon
Claiming His Secret Royal Heir	Nina Milne
Sleigh Ride with the Single Dad	Alison Roberts
A Firefighter in Her Stocking	Janice Lynn
A Christmas Miracle	Amy Andrews
Reunited with Her Surgeon Prince	Marion Lennox
Falling for Her Fake Fiancé	Sue MacKay
The Family She's Longed For	Lucy Clark
Billionaire Boss, Holiday Baby	Janice Maynard
Billionaire's Baby Bind	Katherine Garbera

MILLS & BOON®
Large Print – October 2017

ROMANCE

Sold for the Greek's Heir	Lynne Graham
The Prince's Captive Virgin	Maisey Yates
The Secret Sanchez Heir	Cathy Williams
The Prince's Nine-Month Scandal	Caitlin Crews
Her Sinful Secret	Jane Porter
The Drakon Baby Bargain	Tara Pammi
Xenakis's Convenient Bride	Dani Collins
Her Pregnancy Bombshell	Liz Fielding
Married for His Secret Heir	Jennifer Faye
Behind the Billionaire's Guarded Heart	Leah Ashton
A Marriage Worth Saving	Therese Beharrie

HISTORICAL

The Debutante's Daring Proposal	Annie Burrows
The Convenient Felstone Marriage	Jenni Fletcher
An Unexpected Countess	Laurie Benson
Claiming His Highland Bride	Terri Brisbin
Marrying the Rebellious Miss	Bronwyn Scott

MEDICAL

Their One Night Baby	Carol Marinelli
Forbidden to the Playboy Surgeon	Fiona Lowe
A Mother to Make a Family	Emily Forbes
The Nurse's Baby Secret	Janice Lynn
The Boss Who Stole Her Heart	Jennifer Taylor
Reunited by Their Pregnancy Surprise	Louisa Heaton

0917 GEN STD LP